A Hole Through The Wind

A Novel Based On True Stories

by

Alan Patterson

© Copyright 2020 by Alan Patterson

Acknowledgments

I want to thank the following people for their support in making my book possible:

Dr. Patrick Brogan of Equiception for generously allowing me to use his photo as part of the cover art;

film producer Robin Bissell for being the first who encouraged me to keep on going;

Andreas Kossak for his very encouraging words, his help with dialog, and his formatting of my book;

and, finally, Suzy Pearce for her outstanding work in editing my manuscript.

Table Of Contents

A Hole Through The Wind   11
About The Author   161

A Hole Through the Wind

A Hole Through the Wind

Morgan Jackson smelled the lovely aroma of approaching rain that was forecast for later in the day.

"The rain always brings back memories," he thought.

He remembered the first time he walked down this very street in front of him. It wasn't easy for a poor black boy in those days, especially for a homeless one like himself. He thanked God that he would never see a day like that again. But he knew if it hadn't been for that fateful day years and years ago, he wouldn't be where he was now.

"God sure works in mysterious ways," he said aloud.

Morgan looked up at the storm clouds and listened to the far-distant thunder.

"Hey, Buddy, I've got to load this truck," a young man called out. "Mr. Jackson? Excuse me..."

Morgan turned back at the commotion behind him. There was his rusty, red Ford pick-up truck, backed up to the loading dock of McCarron Feed & Hardware. And there was a young man in overalls trying to toss a heavy sack of fertilizer into the truck's bed. But Buddy, Morgan's scruffy Jack Russel mix, would not allow it. It was, after all, Buddy's truck, and he strutted around, barking and growling, defending every inch of it.

Morgan rushed over to Buddy and rubbed the dog's snout. "You know you're the boss, but now let the young man do his work, okay? We've got to get home soon."

Buddy stopped barking and wagged his tail. The young man tossed the heavy sack, happy to let go of the weight.

Morgan scratched his head. "I still marvel at this small town, as if I had never seen it before."

The young man shook his head. "But you've lived here all your life, Mr. Jackson. Haven't you?"

"Not quite."

The young man looked puzzled. "Well, it's all loaded, Sir… I hope you don't get caught in that thundershower."

"Rain I can handle." Morgan waved at the young man and got behind the wheel of his truck. Buddy jumped in after him. Morgan fired up the old Ford, and Buddy stuck his snout out into the wind.

"See you next week, Mr. Jackson." The young man wiped his brow and walked back into the store.

Morgan and Buddy took the truck down Main Street. Everyone waved hello and Buddy enjoyed the attention.

"You know, Buddy, the first time I was here in this little town, it wasn't like it is now. I don't mean just the new storefronts and paved roads." Morgan shrugged. "I guess, it takes a long time for people to change."

Morgan turned down a long dirt road leading out of town. It was lined with old hickory trees, planted a long time ago with thoughts of the future. Morgan slowed down next to a white fence and came to a stop. "Look, Buddy, this is where it all started."

Morgan pointed across the field. "I was way over yonder on the other side of the pasture that day."

Buddy stuck his head out the window.

"In the back of the feed cart was your great-granddaddy, whose name was Buddy, too."

A large, flying grasshopper landed on a fence post right in front of Morgan.

"Well, all I could hear that day was the hum of the tractor, but I saw the two brothers running. They were running a hole through the wind. That sure was a long time ago. We had better move along now, though. Remember, we have special company coming today."

Back home, Morgan walked over to his favorite rocker on the wooden porch. Buddy followed on his heels. "This is the time of year I love the most; when mares are getting ready to foal." Morgan sat down and reached for Buddy, to rub him between the ears. "We have the perfect place to watch them from here, don't we? Me in this old rocker and you on that old rug."

Buddy leaned up against Morgan's leg.

"You can see for miles. Look, there are the old barns and the training track with that big pond in the middle. We used that a lot, you know. Maybe we'll go fishing tomorrow."

Buddy looked up at him, panting softly and smiling.

Morgan smiled back.

"I can see hundreds of mares and their babies from here. The mares love to roam and graze and the babies love to run and play. That I know for sure. Some of the old trees are gone. But I'll never get tired of what this place smells like. It's that smell of wild tobacco. The one that still grows along the fence over there. And there are those beautiful old Hickory trees along my dirt road. I imagine this is exactly what Heaven looks like."

He ran his spindly fingers through his thinning shock of gray hair, then he rubbed his aging eyes. Buddy stretched and wagged his tail.

Morgan stood up. "Well, lookie there,

Buddy! Here they come!"

A tan and brown station wagon made its way up the road to the old farm house.

Morgan slapped the dust from his overalls and waved as the station wagon pulled up in front of the porch. "Hi, Bill! Hello, Margie!"

The man behind the wheel rolled down his window. "Hi, Dad!"

Margie, riding passenger, waved back at him.

"Where are my two little rascals?"

Right on cue, ten-year-old Steve, and seven-year-old Jimmy, came flying out of the car before it even stopped.

"Hey, Grandpa! Hi, Grandpa! Hey, we've got something for you!"

Bill and Margie climbed out of the car behind the boys, shaking their heads at all that youthful energy.

Jimmy and Steve bounded onto the porch and plopped down an old cardboard box right in front of Morgan.

But Morgan took it slow. He made a point of first walking over to hug his daughter-in-law and then his son.

"That's a nasty storm down the road," Morgan said, looking up at the sky.

"I know, Dad," Bill replied, "I wasn't sure we were going to outrun it and get here in time."

"Guess what we brought you, Grandpa!" Steve begged.

Morgan smiled.

"Come on, Grandpa. Please!" Jimmy pleaded.

Morgan chuckled, "I sure hope there's a pecan pie in there."

"No, there's something better," Steve grinned at Jimmy. "Guess again, Grandpa!"

"Okay, okay." Morgan's eyes twinkled as he squatted down and peeked into the box. There was a stack of old horserace win pictures, yellowing newspaper clippings, and a dried-up rose in a mason jar.

Jimmy grabbed the jar and held it up. "What's the old flower doing in this jar, Grandpa?"

"It came off a blanket of roses that hung around a real champion's neck, and *let me see..." Morgan took a long look, without saying a word.*

"It's at the bottom, Grandpa!"

Morgan took his time.

To hurry things along, they carefully sifted through it until, at last, they came up with the prize they were looking for.

Morgan was stunned. "Oh, my goodness! That's my diary! I thought it was long gone. This is the last thing my mother gave me."

The boys handed him the book, their eyes eagerly searching his.

Morgan stared at the old diary. His hands shook. "Mother told me, 'One day you will be glad you wrote your life down. Keep a diary and someday it will keep you... just take life a day at a time, and if you miss writing in it one day, it's okay.' "

He looked up at the boys, Bill, and Margie. "I haven't seen this diary... let's see... in over fifty years, I think."

He sat back down as if his legs had suddenly given way.

The boys clapped and yelled, "Read it, read it, Grandpa!"

Morgan took a deep breath. "All right, all right, simmer down! I will, I will. But first, I want to know where your dad found all this stuff."

Bill smiled. "A 'Mrs. Johnson' tracked me down. Her mother was Jane Salerno, but you should know her by her maiden name, Harley... Jane Harley and her dad was John."

Morgan nodded. "I know that! I've thought about them often after they moved away. Oh, I remember now. I stored this stuff with her a long time ago. I always meant to get it from her, but then she moved and I guess life just got in the way. Mr. John is the man that sold me this old house. The last time I saw Jane was at Mr. John's funeral along about twenty years ago. Jane and I just sort of lost touch after she got married and moved to England." Morgan looked up at his son. "How did you get it?"

"Well, I hate to tell you this, Dad," Bill said, "but Mrs. Johnson told me that her mother died in a riding accident a couple months ago."

"Oh, no," Morgan said. His family could see that his eyes were wavering from *the tears that sprang to them.*

"I am so sorry to hear that, son."

"Mrs. Johnson told me that her mother died just the way she would have wanted," Bill said, consoling his father.

"That is true," Morgan replied, wiping his eyes, "Very true."

"And, Mrs. Johnson found this box in her mother's house with a note saying it was yours," Bill went on, "She looked up my number, thinking I was you. Mrs. Johnson and her whole family still want to meet you one day. She said her mother talked so much about you. Growing up, she always considered you family. Mrs. Johnson said her mom also told her that she didn't think she would've made it without you."

"Oh, I don't know about that," Morgan said, "She definitely gave me too much credit. Jane was always so sweet; such a good friend. I'm so sorry to know that she's gone."

Morgan smiled sadly, remembering. He opened his dusty, crackled old diary, still amazed it had been found.

"Please, Grandpa, read what's on that

page!"

"There isn't much writing, yet."

Morgan showed little Jimmy and Steve, so they could see for themselves. Then he turned back to the first page.

A bolt of lightning sliced through the treetops. It was followed by the biggest explosion of thunder the little boys had ever heard. Then, the rain fell from the heavens like a blanket of darkness. The boys moved closer to their grandpa.

Morgan, feeling the quietness, spoke slowly. "Look at the horses in the field! Some are still eating, some are looking around, and others run around with their tails up, unsure what's going on."

Morgan's grandsons moved up to his legs on either side of him, resting their chins on his knees.

"Living my life with all those horses, I've figured out that they are all like teenagers. I mean from the time they're babies till they're almost too old to eat. Some are very brave, some shy, some have overcome very hard things in life, but none of them are too old to play and enjoy life."

Morgan marveled *at the two boys on*

his knees, then looked to his son and daughter-in-law.

"I'm so glad you all came all this way to see me. I've been so very lonely here now that my Edna is gone. It's just me and Buddy nowadays."

Morgan roughed up Steve's hair and petted Jimmy's. "I hope you two knotheads can come to spend a summer with me so we can go fishing and I can show you a thing or two about horses. Just today, I stopped at that fence over there. I had to think about the two brothers that went on to become world champions. One was big and the other small."

"Grandpa, are you going to tell us about them?"

Morgan smiled. "Well, I think we might hear about them in this book." He cracked the spine of his stiff, old diary and started remembering.

December 1st

I was wet and cold without money or job. I remember that day, so long ago. I was about fifteen or so. My dad had died and my mother said I should go out on my own; that she and my sis would be heading back to Texas. They were going to live with her aunt.

It was cold and rainy that day. I got lucky and caught a ride with an old trucker who dropped me off not too far from here. All I knew then was that I was in the middle of Kentucky. This place was a one-horse town then, and it's not much bigger now. The trucker had to turn down another road up ahead, so he let me out and wished me luck.

I got out of the truck with my suitcase when he asked me if I would like the other half of his sandwich. He didn't need all of it since he'd be home soon with his family, and his wife was cooking him his favorite meal. I thanked him and put the sandwich, which was wrapped in wax paper, in my pocket. I think it was roast beef and gravy.

I walked around town, from place to place, hopping over mud puddles. I tried to get a job doing anything, anywhere, but nobody had anything I could do for them. Some people were saying no before I even asked them.

A bright flash of lightning streaked across the sky, and a clap of thunder boomed. Once it was all quiet again, Morgan continued.

I was getting drenched and cold from that rain. What was worse, it was getting late, and I had no place to sleep. I didn't know where to turn. I could only pray that something good would happen soon. Real soon.

The temperature dropped fast from that rain, and I needed a place to get out of it. All I saw was a big old lumber truck that had a bunch of boards sticking out the back of it. So, I squatted under it.

Across from me I saw a small, drenched white dog near the back tire. He was shaking something awful. His eyes were uncertain and afraid, his ribs were sticking out, and his white fur was matted with mud. He was too scared and hungry to growl at me.

I could see our breaths. I knew that if he had found some dry porch to crawl under, someone might have thrown him at least some scraps. But now it was every man for himself, and if he did find a place I wasn't too sure if he'd share it with me.

I'd never felt so alone in my life. It was the kind of loneliness that you feel deep in your bones. Nobody wanted me that day. It hurt so bad that I couldn't even cry. I had to keep going because I knew if I'd given up, I'd disappear from the world like clouds over a mountain.

That's when I remembered the sandwich and pulled it out of my pocket. I was going to eat it when that dog's ears shot up as soon as he got a whiff of it. I tore it in half, put it on the wax paper, and sat it over by him. He ate it in one bite. When he was trying to lick the last of the gravy, the paper slid all over the place. So, I put my hand on the corner of the paper to hold it for him. He licked every inch of it.

Just as it was getting dark, an old white pickup truck came by, "Rainbow Farms" painted on the door. I scrambled from beneath the lumber truck as the white man inside drove by me. I was looking at him, and he was looking at me. I was willing him to stop. I was hoping he was the answer to my prayers! But he kept on going. Once again I felt the sting of loneliness that comes only when you get rejected. As I turned to seek refuge under the lumber truck once again, I heard the pickup slide to a stop, grind some gears, fumble to catch reverse, then slowly back up.

My prayers had been answered! I almost slipped and fell down a bunch of times running in the mud up to that truck. He rolled down his window and asked me if I was looking for work.

"Yes!" I squawked, louder than I'd intended to, and he said, "hop in." As we started to drive off, the man must have looked at the lumber truck through his rearview mirror, because he stopped and said, "Hey, you forgot your dog. Better go grab him before he washes away."

I sat stunned for a moment.

"Go on, then," the man said. "It's ok to bring him."

I jumped out of the pickup, ran back to the lumber truck, and called, "Here, Buddy." He came running, jumped up in my arms, and I stuck him in my jacket as if he had done this every day of his life. That's when I knew that I had me my own dog.

As we were driving away, the man said his name was John Harley. I told him my name was Morgan Jackson, and that the dog's name was, well,... Buddy! And Buddy was shaking like only a dog can shake.

"He was the first of many Buddies I've had." Morgan pointed to Buddy at his feet. "The one I've told you about was his great, great-granddaddy. So I guess you can consider him Buddy IV."

Mr. John asked me if I had ever worked with horses before. I lied and said that I had. I don't think he believed me, but he said 'fine' all the same.

He told me the temperature would drop so low at night that icy rain would coat everything. It was that time of the year. God forbid if man or beast got caught in it! Over the years, he had lost a couple of horses in this kind of ice rain before he had a chance to get them into the barn.

Then, he told me I could have supper with him and his daughter Jane.

Pretty soon I started to warm up. I looked into my jacket so that I could see my new dog sleeping. He must have felt me watching him, because he looked up at me and said, "Thanks."

"You can't fool me, Grandpa!" said Jimmy. "Dogs don't talk."

"Yes, they can. They talk with their

eyes."

"Okay, Grandpa."

"Where was I?"

"In Mr. John's truck!"

"Yes, back in the cabin of that truck. After Buddy said 'thanks.' Well..." Morgan winked at Jimmy.

Mr. John was telling me the history of all the farms that we were passing. I saw the pretty white fences and emerald green pastures. Even though the windows were foggy, I could see that Kentucky was a beautiful place, and I could hardly wait 'til spring.

I'd never seen green grass grow in the winter. I thought about growing up in Texas, where there was nothing but barb wire, windmills, and sand. And, there wasn't anything for the cows to eat during a drought, except cactus.

"Grandpa, cows don't eat cactuses, do they?" asked Steve.

"Well, in a drought there's not much grass to eat, so they're forced to eat anything that doesn't move," Morgan said, *"My dad and mom would walk around*

with propane tanks on their backs and burn the stickers off the cactus. The cows would crowd around and wait for them to get done. Then, the cows would push in as soon as mom and dad backed off.

"Some real hungry cows ended up with their lips full of stickers. They'd swell up and the cows would drool because they didn't wait. I never did figure out how those cows knew we were helping them."

Jimmy put his hand on Steve's shoulder. "Let Grandpa go on. So, you're still in Mr. John's truck..."

Morgan took a deep breath.

Anyway, we turned down the road that you just came down and ended up at this very house. That's when I met Mr. John's daughter, Jane. I could tell right off she was a kind girl. I was so ashamed that I was tracking mud into their home, but all she was worried about was that I was soaked to the bone. And when I opened my suitcase, she saw that everything else I owned was wet, even this diary. That's when she got me some of her grandfather's clothes to wear.

Jane saw that Buddy was also a mess and asked me if she could give him a little rinse. She put him in the sink, and he got a warm bath. Afterward, she wrapped him in a big towel and put him by the fireplace with some chow. I looked around the house while Buddy was getting his spa treatment. I saw the walls were filled with horse pictures and quite a few trophies sat on the mantel of the fireplace.

We had a great supper that night. I stuffed myself while Mr. John went on to tell me how he and his dad had built this farm to breed racehorses.

Some years before, he and his dad had had some luck with an old sire that made them enough money to buy this farm. But, Mr. John lost almost everything he owned because his wife was sick for a long time. He didn't have insurance to cover the hospital expenses and was forced to sell the farm and all that went with it.

He sold it to an evil, rotten man named Craig. But Mr. John got to keep one old, cheap mare that Craig didn't want to feed.

There were other buyers who wanted the farm, but that Craig fellow scared them all off. He basically stole the farm, getting the whole place for bottom dollar. Then he turned around and fired everyone who worked there and forced Mr. John to stay on as farm manager. So, Mr. John and Jane had to move out of their big house and into this small place, which his dad had lived in.

Mr. John told me it would have broke his heart to leave the farm, and he had Jane to worry about. I know now Mr. John was hoping to get his place back one day.

After supper, he told me I could stay with them and sleep in the tack room in the barn. That's where all the saddles, bridles, and smelly horse blankets were kept. It leaked a little, he said, but I would be okay.

Mr. John also warned me to watch out for that Craig fellow. He was a very prejudiced man and didn't like what he called 'colored people' around him. He thought all they wanted was to rob him blind.

I remember walking over to the barn with Mr. John. As we walked down the shedrow, it was as black as ink, the kind of place bats like. When we entered the barn, I also got my first real smell of horses, even though I'd been around horses before. I loved it.

Mr. John had a lantern, and Buddy and I saw some horses that were sleeping at the back of their stalls. A few stuck their heads out to see what was going on. The light from the lantern entered their inky stalls. As the light moved, the shadows from the bars made the horses look like they had stripes.

I was a little spooked when some of them would reach out through the dark. They'd touch me with their fuzzy noses and snort hot air down the back of my neck, making me jump. We stopped at the end of the shedrow and Mr. John pointed to a horse in the last stall. He told me her name was Dancing Home, and that she was the best mare of the farm and probably of all Kentucky. He said she was due to foal at any time and asked me to keep an ear on her. If she went into labor, I was to come and get him fast.

Mr. John helped me fix my cot. He told me he'd come and get me at feeding time, which was 3:30 am, and said goodnight.

I crawled into my bed and looked around at all the horse equipment. I could smell the medicine bottles. Finally, I started to warm up. I looked over at Buddy. He was all wrapped up in a towel. I told him how wonderful this day had turned out to be.

December 25th

You know, I remember that Christmas, my first Christmas at the farm. It was the best night of my life. After chores, I cleaned up and went over to the house. When I walked in, I saw a big turkey dinner waiting for me, and I could smell the pumpkin pie in the oven. I could also smell the pine Christmas tree Jane had set up. And when I looked over at the tree, I saw some gifts under it. I had seen wrapped gifts before but never as pretty as what I saw under that tree. I didn't want to be rude looking at the gifts, so I excused myself to go to the bathroom. And as I slowly walked by, I saw that the biggest gift had my name on it. When I was in the restroom, I realized I didn't have a gift for them. I still feel guilty about that.

We had a great dinner that night, and after helping with the dishes and cleaning the table, we moved to the tree. Jane reached over and handed me that big gift box with all the pretty paper and ribbons on it. I slowly opened it, trying not to tear the paper or hurt the ribbon. I never had new, store-bought clothes before. All my clothes had been hand-me-downs or whatever I could find, but in that box was a brand-new jacket and a bundle of white cotton socks. What more does a man need?

I recall that mare, also, the one called Dancing Home. All the other mares had already foaled, and Dancing Home was last. I sure loved that mare. She was about the sweetest thing you can imagine. To move her from the pasture back to the barn, I only needed to put a carrot in my back pocket and she'd follow me anywhere.

She was the mare Mr. John really wanted to keep in the bankruptcy sale. He told me he and his dad bred her mother to Big Jake, and that she was the last mare Big Jake ever bred. Mr. John always thought she was going to be a champion. She had won five races in a row just before the Kentucky Derby, but an injury kept her out of that race. Later on, Mr. John had to help that Craig fellow make a deal with another farm to get her bred by their top sire.

About two in the morning, Buddy started barking, so I got up to see what he was barking about. I looked around and saw Dancing Home, was in labor. I turned around in a panic with the idea to run and alert Mr. John, but when I turned I ran head-on into him.

He was checking on his mare Little Bess and saw that she was in hard labor, too. So he was coming to get me to help when he saw that

Dancing Home was also in the same state. Both mares where in trouble at the same time, but he stayed with Dancing Home.

Mr. John told me to get Jane. I was also to run over to the big house where Craig lived. I was supposed to tell him that Dancing Home was in labor, and Mr. John had called the vet Craig wanted him to use. But that vet didn't want to come right away; he said he'd come later in the morning when the weather eased up.

I ran as fast as I could and told Craig what Mr. John asked me to say. And man, was that Craig furious, yelling at me to get my black ass off his porch. It was the first time I ever spoke to him.

Jane was already there when I came back. Dancing Home was all sweaty. I couldn't figure out how the mare could be so sweaty when there was freezing rain outside. That's when that Craig fellow drove up in his new car and came waddling his bulk down the shed row. He left the barn door wide open again. With a big cigar in his mouth, he hollered at Mr. John for having sent a colored boy to talk to him, at his house no less. Just who in the hell did Mr. John think he was? Mr. John just ignored him, keeping his attention firmly focused on Dancing Home.

A few minutes later, Dancing Home popped out the biggest colt I had ever seen. He was so grand to look at. There were grins of happiness shared among all of us. But when I looked to Mr. John, I saw that he was still watching Dancing Home. She still didn't look right. She looked like she was still in labor. And guess what? She was. Mr. John eased his hands inside the mare to help turn another baby that was sideways. It was a good thing he did that because she would've died otherwise.

Five minutes later, she slowly eased out another colt, but this one was a runt. That Craig started screeching and directed all of his anger at Mr. John. He wanted to know how this could've happened. Mr. John told him that Craig's vet was a lazy man who didn't know beans about the breeding end of horses, but was a good golfer.

That's when Craig, that bastard, did something that shocked me. He told Mr. John to pick up the runt and put him in the outside pen. That Craig fellow was hoping the icy rain weather would take care of his problem, and we were to never tell anyone about what just happened with the twins. If anyone did ever find out, he'd fire us all. He threatened that Mr. John and Jane would have to move out of their house, and that he'd ruin anyone who ever told. Finally, he turned to me and yelled, "that goes for your sorry black ass and Jane's, too."

Jimmy's jaw dropped. "Grandpa, why was that man so mad?"

"Well, I didn't know then, but no one really wants twins in the racehorse business. They're almost always runts, or sometimes they get really sick and die. But most people think their genes are split. It's also hard on the mare that some of them die."

"But this runt was alive and Dancing Home, too!"

"Jimmy, that's racehorse business," Morgan tried to soothe his distressed grandson. "Had the vet caught this early, he would've pinched one of the fetuses. That way, the other one could grow to normal size, and, most importantly, save the life of the mare. But the vet didn't catch it, so that Craig yelled how he was ruined for the year, how his investors would never sit still for this, and that he would look like an idiot. He'd have to wait another full year for one of her babies, which meant having to pay for another breeding fee."

"Grandpa, why didn't the vet see that she was going to have twins?" Steve asked.

"Good question, Steve. Mr. John told

me later that he thought he knew how it happened though he couldn't prove it. He said, 'Do you remember the time when we were examining the mares? To see which mares were pregnant and which mares needed to be bred again?'

"This idiot vet had checked nineteen mares that day with only two mares left, Dancing Home and my mare. He said he had a golf game that day, and that he'd check the last two the next day. Because that Craig left another gate open, we were busy chasing down loose horses, when the vet came back. The vet didn't care that we were dealing with that mishap. He demanded the last two horses be brought to him right away. I told him he'd have to wait because we were chasing loose horses, and he got mad.

"When I left, the vet went out to the barn and grabbed what he thought was Dancing Home and Little Bess, Mr. John's mare. They were the last two mares to get checked. He did a quick check on the wrong two mares because Dancing Home and Little Bess were in the other barn. I didn't figure this out till later."

"Grandpa, what did John and you do

with the little baby? Did you really put him in that outside pen?" Jimmy tried not to cry.

"Well... Being a father, Mr. John's main priority was Jane. He couldn't afford to get fired and lose everything. So, Mr. John slowly picked up that little baby. I saw him and Jane look at each other. Her eyes were filling up with tears. Both of them didn't want to do this.

"Jane knew that that little baby would be put in the outside pen only a few feet from her on the other side of the wall. There it would die a slow death. Jane stayed with Big Brother and the mare in the warm barn. I helped Mr. John by opening the frozen barn door, but before I could help any further, Jane busted out crying. I just couldn't get over what was happening before my eyes.

"The barn door was stuck from all that icy rain, and the floor was slippery. When I finally did get that door open, a blast of freezing air hit me, almost blowing me over. When I got the outside pen open, I wished I had my gloves on. Mr. John put that little baby down in a pen of mud and freezing rain.

"That little colt spent the first minutes of his life in the total darkness. He staggered around up to his knees in icy mud, freezing to death. We tried to erect a quick, plywood lean-to to help him, but the little guy didn't understand. He kept trying to walk around in the mud only to keep falling down."

"Did he die?"

"Now, Steve, don't get ahead of me. Just settle down and listen."

Mr. John put the baby brother down in the outside pen and told me he would check on his own mare, Little Bess. She was in a small barn next door. I watched that Craig fellow spin his tires in the mud and speed away from the farm. He never gave a second thought to the cruelty he had ordered Mr. John to carry out.

But Mr. John was only in his mare's stall for a moment until he came flying past me and opened that outside pen. He picked up the little baby and yelled for me to open the stall next to his mare. That's where he carried the little colt.

I looked into his mare's stall and saw the reason why. Mr. John hadn't been in there to help with his own mare's birth, and her foal was stillborn.

Dead.

    Mr. John and I rubbed the little runt down with some rags and straw, trying to dry him off and warm him up a little. I recall that he was definitely going to be a bay. You know what that means, boys? It means that he was a reddish-brown color with black legs, mane, and tail. We carried the other dead colt outside and rubbed the afterbirth from the dead colt onto the bay runt. Now Mr. John carried the little brother into the stall to his new momma. She slowly walked over to him, smelled him, and licked him. She wrapped her head and neck around him and pulled him over for his first warm breakfast.

    As the mare adopted the runt, I thought Mr. John was still standing there with me, watching the miracle. But when I looked around, I couldn't find him. I found him outside in the cold with that dead colt. He laid him in the outside pen where the little runt had just been. All of his high hopes for a good baby of his own were gone. He would have to wait a year for another chance.

    I walked up to Mr. John and saw that he was crying. I didn't know what to say, and I didn't want to say the wrong words, so I decided to not say anything. But I did something that surprised even me. I took Mr. John's hand and led him back inside the barn so he wouldn't get sick in the rain.

"What happened next?" Steve looked at his brother who was also trying not to cry.

Well, the next day that Craig fellow walked around the farm and saw the frozen colt in the outside pen. He thought it was the little runt. His eyes lit up because he figured that this part of his problem was over. The question was what to do with his surviving colt. The big brother was extremely well-bred, but Craig was scared that someone would find out that his colt was a twin and he'd only get a fraction of what he invested. Besides, if anyone ever found out what he ordered Mr. John to do to the other twin, he could've gone to jail or maybe even lose the farm. So, he figured "buyer beware" because for Craig it was never about the horse, anyway; it was all about the money.

Originally, he planned to wait till Big Brother was a two-year-old so he could get top dollar at the sale, but now he was concerned a defect might show up. In fact, he was down-right paranoid He decided that he would sell him right away as a weanling. He'd make way less money, but he would be out of his dilemma.

The next day, everyone quietly did their chores,

working with their heads down. At supper time, Mr. John finally spoke up. He said that this would been the last time he'd ever let that bastard Craig tell him to do something that he knew was wrong.

Then Jane asked what he was going to do with the baby runt.

"Well, for one thing," Mr. John said, "that little guy will never make it as a racehorse."

He went on to say that the little baby was way too small. In any case, we would take care of him as our own and, when he got older, we would find a good home for him.

"He might make a good riding horse for someone," Mr. John said.

Jimmy, relieved, wiped his eyes, trying to hide the tears from his little brother.

"Mr. John was a good man, wasn't he?" Jimmy said.

"That he was," Morgan nodded, "An honest man, like my own dad. Your kids' great-grandpa. I think that's why I admired Mr. John so much. He was kind and honest."

I was born in Colorado City, Texas where my

dad and mom were sharecroppers. They moved around a lot in those days, trying to find work doing anything they could. My dad mostly farmed. He didn't want me to grow up like him. He wanted me to go to school and get an education. Even though I went to school, I still helped my dad pick cotton.

One day, my dad made an offer. My little sister and I could go to the picture show if I could pick one hundred pounds of cotton in a day. My mother made me a little cotton-picking sack out of a 50 lb. potato sack with a strap to go over my shoulder.

Now, I was only in the first grade then, so that sack was as big as me! Anyway, I took a running to the field. I was going to show my dad how fast I was! The first hour, I picked really fast, but, as the sun got hotter, I was sweating and slowing down fast. My hands were raw, so I started cheating. I would put green bolls of cotton in with the white cotton. The green ones are twice as heavy as the white ones but are not ready to be picked.

That still didn't make my sack feel any heavier, and I started putting hands of sand in with the cotton. I checked every once in a while, to see if my dad was looking. But, he didn't.

Around lunch break, my dad said, "Let's see how much you've picked so far." He put my cotton sack on the scales. And all the time he was looking at the scales, he patted both sides of my sack until all the sand had gathered at the bottom.

Then, he pulled out his pocketknife. He poked a small hole in my sack and let all that sand drain out. He said it looked like I was dragging my sack too close to the ground and getting way too many green bolls in there.

My cotton sack went from nineteen pounds to ten! And not once, did my dad say I was cheating. Years later, he told me that he'd "filled" his sack the same as I did!

Now, I only had half a day to make that hundred pounds. Even though my dad gave me some of his cotton, my sack only weighed thirty-eight pounds at the end of the day.

Still, he allowed my little sister and I to go to the picture show after supper. But I was so tired, all I could do after supper was sleep.

By the time I was in second grade, I was driving a tractor. I would sit in my dad's lap, learning the gears and how to shift. At first, I cried because I was scared. I couldn't steer that tractor straight in all that deep sand. But my dad kept telling me everything was okay, and that I was doing a good job.

By the end of summer, I was good at driving that tractor. I even wanted to drive it to school and show my friends that I could drive all by myself.

One of my friends showed me how to speed-shift that tractor and make the front of it pop up, doing a little wheelie. I could only practice speed-shifting and driving fast when we parked the tractor in the shed at the end of the day. I had about three miles of hard road. At first, my dad would ride on the back of the tractor with me, and my mom would follow behind in the car. As my dad saw I could do ok by myself, he told my mother she didn't need to help us anymore, that he and I could do it all.

To trick my dad into not following me in the car, I would gradually slow down the tractor till my dad got tired. I knew he would pass me and wait at the gate. As soon as he was out of sight, I would stop the tractor, put it in first gear, rev the motor, and pop the clutch. The front of the tractor felt like it was flying up.

I didn't understand then that this was one of the ways to get killed on a tractor. So, if you ever get the bright idea to do something like that, you just turn and walk away from it.

My dad had a great sense of humor. He was always laughing. He'd always sing the same stupid song about three hot tomalleys and how one always got stuck. I sure miss hearing that laugh of his.

"What happened to him?" Steve asked.

"Shhh!" Jimmy frowned, "Let him finish!"

Morgan chuckled a little.

Well, he was the hardest working man I've ever known. He started work before the sun came up and came home way after it went down.

One day, I noticed that he didn't look right, pale and thinner than usual. His appetite started to fail and he seemed to have to sit down more often than he ever had to before. That went on for almost a year. Sometime later, I walked in on a serious conversation between my mom and dad. That's when my mom told me he had cancer and he didn't have long to live. I was thirteen then.

I quit school to do my dad's job after that. At night, I had long talks with him, and he was so hard on me it seemed like I couldn't do anything right. Finally, my mother took me aside. She told me the reason he was so hard on me was that he only had a short time to live. He wanted me to grow up to be a good man, fast.

I never really knew if God answers prayers, but I prayed every day that God would heal him. But my dad got weaker and weaker, until finally I asked God if he would please take him. I didn't want him to suffer anymore. Before he died, he told me to be proud of who I was. He said I was unique with a special purpose in life and I should always remember that nobody could ever take away that I was a good man. I could only do that to myself.

The next night around three in the morning, my mother woke me and said my dad was in a coma. And I remember, as stood there as the preacher was praying, I saw him take his last breath.

A couple of days after we buried my dad, the landowner told us to leave. We lived in his house while we did his cotton, and now he wanted to move in another family. That's why my mother and sister moved back to Texas, and I hit the road.

It was very hard for a young black man to find work back then. But I kept going around picking up work for a couple of years until one day I hit rock bottom. That's when I caught the ride with that trucker, who dropped me off down the road.

Jimmy was curious. "Grandpa, did you have horses when you were growing up?"

Morgan shook his head. "Naw, we never owned a horse. But the time I got to ride the most was when I was about five or six. We were on a farm, and the man who owned the farm-raised cotton, cows, and some horses."

One day, my dad asked that owner why we were plowing the cotton under after the picking was over. Couldn't we just let the cows and horses eat what was left? It would sure fatten them up a little. After that, we had to herd the cows on foot, and all that walking around was too much.

So, my dad would catch one of the horses. He'd pull out some bailing twine, which he always carried in his pocket. He tied that twine around the horse's bottom jaw, Indian-style. Then, he swung up, reached down, and pulled me up.

That way, we would herd the cows on horseback. The owner wanted to also ride the horses, but he couldn't figure out how my dad caught them. So, he tried using his truck to chase the horses into a pen, but all he did was scatter them and stir up a lot of dust!

Steve asked eagerly, "How did your dad catch them?"

"I asked my dad one day how he did it, and he told me that every time he saw the

horses, he'd give them a gift."

Steve looked confused.

"Well, people nowadays call it a 'treat.' Back then, my dad gave them something they already ate or something they couldn't reach like a piece of grass from the other side of the fence.

"You know what I did after I learned that? I was too little to get on horses by myself, so I'd get some hay or grass and put it down in front of them. When they would drop their heads to eat, I'd swing a leg over their neck, and they would pick up their heads. That would let me slide down onto their backs. Then I'd quickly spin around and face the front. My dad always thought that was funny. He was a natural horseman. I still admire that." Morgan's eyes shined as he remembered.

One day, my dad took us kids and mom to a rodeo, because before he and mom got married, he'd followed the rodeo circuit. He rode bucking horses and bulls, and he roped. But, when he got married, he started working in the fields so he'd have a steady paycheck and not get busted up so much. Anyway, after the rodeo that day, there was a crowd gathering around an old, beat-up horse trailer. I could hear cracking and popping sounds and a lot of yelling.

When we walked up, we saw a man whipping his horse into a trailer. To me, it looked way too small for that horse. The man used his bullwhip to hit the horse on the back legs. I heard my mom say, "Oh my God, look at that horse's back legs! He's cutting them to shreds!" Blood was already everywhere, and each time the man whipped the horse on his back legs, it just stood there and quivered. Before the man could hit his horse again, my dad pushed me to the side and grabbed that man's arm.

The man swung around, and I thought he was going to hit my dad. Then, before the man could say a word, my dad said, "Can I help you load your horse, sir?" And before that man could say or do anything, my dad grabbed the horse's lead rope. He led him around in a couple of circles, then walked into the trailer first. Once inside, he gently encouraged the horse to follow him. At first the horse balked, but my dad finally talked him into coming inside the trailer with him.

Some men from the crowd closed the trailer's gate and my dad climbed out the side door. My dad walked right up to the man and handed him his lead rope. He told the man that it looked like his horse would need a lot of doctoring.

Then he gathered us together and we walked away. I heard a lady behind us say, "Did you see that?" And there was another man saying, "It's a good thing that black man didn't touch me, or I would've ...." I turned around, and the man saw me looking at him. He looked away from my accusing eyes and walked off. We headed back to our old car, and my sister and I tried looking back at what had just happened, but dad kept turning us around. It seemed to me that everyone was watching us. Only years later did I finally realized how brave my dad had been for doing what he did.

"Wow, Great-Grandpa was cool!" Both grandsons nodded their heads.

Morgan laughed at their enthusiasm. "Yes, I guess he was." His eyes misted a little. He looked down to hide the expression on his face.

"Did that horse's legs ever get better?" Steve wanted to know.

"I asked my dad one day about that horse, and all he said was some people shouldn't have kids or animals."

Morgan leaned back in his rocking chair and continued.

February 15th

    Back then, I worked hard from three-thirty a.m. till we got the work done. But it was good work. I went to bed tired and always hated getting up early, especially when it was cold. Still, working with Mr. John made it worthwhile.

    And I tried hard to stay away from that Craig. He always glared at me, made bigoted remarks, and yelled for me to get more chores done. I thought if he wanted more work done, he should've hired more help.

    Buddy growled at him one time, and when he tried to kick him, that Craig slipped and fell on his butt. I told Mr. John and Jane about it at supper, and we laughed so hard we thought our sides would split. I just loved that Miss Jane. She was so sweet. Mr. John said, "She's just like her mom. She understands the importance and responsibility of running a breeding farm. And, she's only fourteen!"

    You see, Mr. John spent his entire life around horses. Everything he knew, he'd learned from his father. Mr. John liked farm work and didn't have any desire to be a trainer at the racetrack. He liked to stay at his farm. There, he could breed his mares, raise the babies, break them, and get them ready for the track.

Mr. John told me a story one time about his dad. He said that his father was a very successful trainer who made a living getting the best out of "cheap" horses. One day, a man came up to his dad and asked him to buy one particular horse at an upcoming two-year-old sale. Mr. John's dad told him the horse was a "good buy." So, the man said, "Okay, you buy the horse, so no one will see me bidding and running the bid up." The day after the sale, the man was upset because he thought the right people weren't bidding on it, so he refused to pay his dad what he owed him and didn't want the horse anymore, either. His dad was stuck with that horse. It almost put him in the poorhouse.

His dad kept working with the horse. He tried to sell him, but when other people heard what happened, nobody wanted him. So, his dad named him Big Jake and put him into training. And boy could that horse run! Big Jake won his first race in a very fast time and he went on to win, again and again, beating some of the top horses at that time. The man who wanted the horse at the sale in the first place now wanted it back, but Mr. John's dad told him to go jump in a lake.

Big Jake made a small fortune for those days and Mr. John's dad used the money to buy this farm, which they named Rainbow Farms. When his racing career was over, that horse went on to produce lots of champion horses.

"Why'd they name it that?" Jimmy asked.

Morgan smiled. "Miss Jane told me one day that when she was a small girl, she asked her grandfather what he was going to call the farm. He told her she could name it. So, after some thought, she said, "I know, Granddad, you told me Big Jake was your pot of gold. When I was little, I used to walk all over this farm looking for that pot of gold, so I want to name this place, Rainbow Farms."

Morgan stood up and pointed across the pasture.

"Look over there, boys, see that big pond?"

Steve and Jimmy stood up to get a better view.

"Mr. John told me the thing that he loved most about this place was that pond. It's set right in the middle of the property *with all of those big hickory trees around it. When they built the training track, they angled it between the trees and were able to keep the pond in the middle.*

"I can see it, Grandpa!" Jimmy was on his toes.

Stevie sat down again.

"Keep on going, Grandpa."

Well, this was an old tobacco farm before he bought it. While most of the tobacco plants had been mowed down, they had let some grow wild along the fence. Mr. John loved the smell of those plants and the trees. In the spring, there isn't a more beautiful place.

It seems like everything blooms around here, even the weeds. Mr. John said, that on nice sunny days, he would put his sick wife in a rowboat. He and Jane would row them out to the middle of the pond. There, his wife would take a nap, and he and Jane would fish as they talked about horses.

Their biggest talk was about their dream to one day breed a foal that would win the Kentucky Derby. Plus, of course, what they would do with all the money they'd win.

"Grandpa, what happen to Jane's

mother?" *Steve wanted to know.*

Well, after I was there for a while, I asked Mr. John what happen to his wife, and he told me. One day, he loaned his truck to someone who needed it, and the man promised that he'd be right back. However, the man stayed in town after he was done and had a few drinks. By the time the man showed up with the truck, Mr. John's wife, who was pregnant, had gone into labor with Jane. When he finally got his wife to the hospital the complications of childbirth proved too much. She never fully recovered.

She had spent years in bed and in a wheelchair. He said she always remained upbeat and supportive, though. He said her quick wit and loving smile was the ingredient that kept the family together, no matter how hard the time got. Mr. John loved her with all his heart and soul, and both he and Jane did everything to make her comfortable.

Unfortunately, her health kept declining, and she finally died. Mr. John and Jane were left to take care of themselves. He grieved for years over her and threw himself into his work.

He told me in private that one day, while packing up his stuff to move out of his home, he came across his dad's pistol, a Colt .357. There was ammo in the drawer, and he pulled it out. He thought he could easily end all he was going through. He'd slowly loaded the pistol and looked at it. But something kept him from it. He didn't know what exactly, but right after he'd put the gun away, he heard Jane calling for him.

Mr. John didn't have any insurance to cover his wife's sickness, so he had to sell the farm and all the horses. But, remember, he kept one old mare.

Morgan thumbed through the pages of the diary, "Let, me see... Oh yes, here it is.... Well, let's see what I wrote... no... not that... here's a girl I met. I will never forget that day."

Jimmy looked around. "Can't we get back to what happened to that little baby?"

Morgan laughed. "Here we go, but I want to come back to that girl. Your dad will love that part."

June 13th

It was the most unusual day I ever saw. Little Brother can run!

> *Steve looked confused. "What does that mean? I thought all horses could run."*
>
> *Morgan smiled. "Yes, that's true, but some can run faster than others. Let me explain."*

Something you boys need to remember is that one thing that little guy was better at than anyone, was opening up gates. I learned that when he let himself out of his stall and I caught him stomping around real close to the house, getting into just about everything. So, we had to be sure to latch a stud chain around the gate to secure it shut.

Since that Craig fellow was so mean, he told Mr. John not to put his colt in the pasture with the other ones. But even though Little Brother was separated from them by a big fence and a gate that was securely latched closed, that little rascal still found a way to run with them. He would wait for them in his corner to come by his side of the fence, then he would run beside them until he had to do a quick stop because his pen was small. Sometimes he had to wait for them for a long time.

One day, when Mr. John, Buddy, and I were out feeding the horses in the pasture, Mr. John stopped the tractor, stood up on the seat, and yelled, "NO, NO, NO!" He almost threw me and Buddy over the side of the feed cart being pulled behind.

Well, at first, I couldn't see what Mr. John was looking at. Then, I saw Little Brother sliding under the fence! It was muddy from rain and he must not have stopped in time while he was running with the other colts, so he skidded, fell, and slid smooth as glass entirely to the other side, where I saw him get up. The other colts walked over and smelled him, including Big Brother.

Now, Big Brother was a bully. His game was to nip and bite the other colts, get them to run, and run them down. Little Brother was no exception. Big Brother took a big ol' bite out of Little Brother's belly. And that's when Little Brother took off. He ran scared because he had never been around any other horse besides his mom, and it must have been a surprise to be greeted in such a way.

All the colts followed in hot pursuit, but the big bully came flying past the pack. Both Big Brother and Little Brother went head-to-head all the way around that big field way in front of the rest of them. Mr. John and I quickly drove to Little Brother's rescue. I don't think the tractor had ever gone that fast before. As we bounded into the pasture, bouncing this way and that in the feed cart, Buddy and I saw all the mares and the colts coming toward us, seeing it was feeding-time. The chase was over, and the real race, the duel, had come to an end.

Good thing, too. We had just scooped up Little Brother and put him back in his own pen with his mother when that Craig drove by with some of his suckers.

I stood in the pen with Little Brother, acting like nothing was out of the ordinary. I let Little Brother lick my hand, then I tugged on his tongue. He sure liked to play that game with me. When he was relaxed and in a good mood, he would let that tongue flop out like a fish and he would want me to pull on it, then he would lick my hand and sometimes my arm.

That Craig fellow drove by all slow, giving me and Little Brother the evil eye.

Morgan paused, secretly loving the anticipation that was so apparent on his grandsons' faces.

"What happened next?" Steve demanded.

"I sure could use some sweet tea and some of that pecan pie that I can smell," Morgan stretched lazily, "I could finish this story the next time you two knot-heads come to see me."

Jimmy turned to his mom. "Mom, please get Grandpa some pie so he can finish the story, pretty please. We want to hear it now. Okay?"

Morgan smiled. "Well then..."

That night at supper, Mr. John and I told Jane what happened with the two brothers. You should have seen her eyes; they were like saucers.

Before that day, Mr. John had been trying to somehow give away Little Brother to a good home. He thought he would be a good riding horse or a jumper for someone. But it seemed like those plans were over. Little Brother could run!

Jane and I were laughing and talking, saying if only things could turn out this well all the time.

Then, I saw Mr. John looking straight ahead, and it got really quiet.

Finally, Mr. John spoke.

"I've worked with baby foals all my life, and I've never seen two colts run that fast. I swear to God, kids, they looked like they could run a hole through the wind, didn't they? We'll just have to wait until he's a two-year-old, then we'll break him, put some training into him, and test him.

"For now, we'll just have to wait. And that's gonna be another year and a half. I've waited for this horse all of my life. What the heck, I'll nominate him for the Kentucky Derby, too. His big brother was just nominated by the new owners yesterday. It only costs a hundred dollars, so why not? I'd love if he was a little bigger for a racehorse. You can't breed heart into a horse, and he's been all heart from since he was born."

Jane and I were floored. We could only stare at each other. Then, we all started grinning and laughing.

"Now, let me tell you about my first girlfriend." Morgan interrupted himself this time.

"No grandpa! Hurry up, and tell us when Little Brother is two and old enough

63

to ride."

"Okay... Say, you sure you don't you want to hear the story about my girlfriend? I bet your dad does."

Morgan's son rolled his eyes.

"Please, we want to hear about Little Brother," Jimmy insisted.

"Oh, alright, let me find it." Morgan fumbled through the diary. "Here we go..."

July 5th

"This was the day when Little Brother was gone and Mr. John and I reckoned he was stolen."

Jimmy jumped up. "What'd you mean?' Someone 'stole' him? How Grandpa?"

"Yes, stolen. You'll see."

Mr. John made plans for the three of us to go to a diner for the Fourth of July. So, we finished our work early and drove to town.

We got back at about 10 p.m. that night, and I went to bed. But I kept hearing a horse whinnying over and over. At about 2 a.m., I couldn't sleep anymore because of all that noise. I got up, and Buddy and I walked out to see what all the fuss was about.

It was a moonless night. I expected to see a coyote or something, only to find it was Little Bess, Little Brother's mom. She was making so much noise and was all worked up. Her head up in the air and she was sweaty all over. She was running around the pen.

At first, I wasn't looking for Little Brother. I thought he was in the back of the pen, somewhere in the dark. But when I began to walk around the pen, trying to calm his momma down, I didn't see Little Brother at all. That's when I realized he was missing. I checked the gate, and it was still locked, the stud chain still securely in place. Someone had taken him. I ran up to this very house and woke up Mr. John.

We doubled back looking everywhere for Little Brother. Mr. John kept asking me over and over if I was sure I had locked the gate. I told him that I knew how good Little Brother was at unlocking gates, so I always double and triple checked. Besides, Little Brother wouldn't have locked his gate once he got out, would he? That stud chain wouldn't latch itself, would it? That's when we saw the tire tracks.

The sheriff arrived first thing in the morning, but all we saw were those truck and trailer tracks. You know, that Craig fellow rarely came out to the farm early, but that morning of all mornings, he came and wanted to know what all the fuss was about. When the sheriff told him that he was there because of a possible stolen horse, he started hollering at Mr. John, saying Mr. John wasn't watching his farm good enough. That is, until he found out it was Mr. John's colt that was stolen. Now that Craig started grinning. He told Mr. John that he didn't want him wasting any of his time looking for that runt. He even said that someone had done Mr. John a favor by stealing him.

We got done early that day, so we drove around to all the other farms to see if anybody had seen Little Brother. The other sad thing was that Mr. John had to tell Jane that Little Brother was stolen. At first, she thought he had opened the gate by himself and was around the farm somewhere. When Mr. John showed her the tire tracks, she started crying, and that made me cry and got me real mad, too. You know, boys, any time Jane got upset about something I ended up getting angry.

We asked the other farms to keep an eye out for our little baby and we put up posters. It was a picture of Little Brother and Jane when he was just a few weeks old. Jane missed activities at school and playing with her friends searching for him. She rode her bike all over the place, looked everywhere, and asked everyone to keep their eyes open. We looked every day for him for the first couple of weeks then less and less, till we finally gave up.

We just couldn't figure out why someone would take Little Brother. After all, they could have taken any of the other high-bred horses on the farm, so why him?

One night, she told us about the last place she had gone to that day. It was Old Tom's place. She walked up to his door and looked around the front of the house. The place was run-down. Then, she heard a baby horse whinnying. She noticed the very dark head of a horse poking around the side of a small shed. That's when Old Tom came flying out the front door and scared her half to death.

"What're you doin' here!" the man demanded.

"I'm looking for a bay baby colt we lost."

Old Tom hurled insults at poor Jane. He told her that it was no wonder we were losing horses the way we ran our place. As she was leaving, that little black baby was making all kinds of noise and commenced to throwing a wild fit. Little did Jane know at the time that it was Little Brother calling her!

"How did you find him, grandpa?"

"We were blessed, Steve. We didn't find him, he found us."

I'll never forget how sad everyone was about losing Little Brother. We looked for him all summer and fall. When winter came, it was going to be a sad Christmas. On Christmas Eve, we talked about many things, but we always ended up talking about Little Brother. Where was he? How was he doing? What could have happened? It was the same old thing over and over. Since it was Christmas Eve, Mr. John allowed me to sleep in on Christmas morning. He would feed the horses.

Just when I turned off my alarm set at 3:30 a.m., I heard pawing and other little noises. At first, I thought it was Mr. John feeding the horses. Then, Buddy barked in a funny way. He wagged his tail, wanting out. So, after a while, I got up to go help Mr. John who I thought was making all that noise. Then, I had the shock of my life as I walked out of my tack room.

There stood a little, ugly black colt. But Little Brother wasn't black, remember? He was a bay, and there's no confusing a black horse with a bay horse. But somehow, I just knew it was Little Brother. First thing he did was stick out his tongue, wanting me to play with it like we used to.

I ran as fast as I could, falling down in the snow, yelling for everyone to get up and come outside. I scared Mr. John half to death. He thought the house or barn was on fire. But all I could do was point and say, "HE'S BACK!!!" Mr. John came running out in just his underpants. He looked at Little Brother, who was a bit bigger now, closely.

"Those sorry bastards," he said. "They dyed him!"

It snowed the last two days, so Mr. John told me to saddle up two pony horses. We were going to follow his tracks to see where they led. We got some warm clothing and took off.

Jane took Little Brother to the barn for a feast of hot mash and a warm bath afterward. It was going to take a while to wash off the black dye.

Mr. John and I went for about 15 miles in the snow, following his little tracks from farm to farm where he stopped and pawed the ground for something to eat. The snow had covered the ground and he couldn't get into any of the fields to eat with the other horses, so he kept moving on. We saw where he spent the night in the snow.

At last, a little farther down the road, we saw where he'd been kept all those months.

Mr. John got off his horse and followed the little tracks to an old shed. He looked inside.

"This is it," was all Mr. John said before he stormed away.

I looked inside and saw that the dye was everywhere – all over the ground and on the sides of the shed. It looked like Little Brother didn't accept the dye job without a fight.

"Who did this?" I called to Mr. John as I trotted after him toward our saddle ponies. "Mr. John, whose place is this?"

Mr. John was up on his pony, ready to hit the road fast.

"It's Old Tom's place," he said. "Hurry up, now. We have to tell the sheriff."

"Old Tom's place? What's Tom's place? Who's Tom?" Jimmy looked like he missed something.

"I remember he was an old coot Mr. John allowed onto the farm. He took our old and moldy hay and fed it to his cows. Later, he started to take our good hay, too. Mr. John warned him that he needed to cut it out, but Old Tom kept on stealing. The last time Mr. John caught him, he forbid him to come back, threatening to tell the law. That's what got Tom so mad."

"Mr. John called the sheriff this time, though. Right, Grandpa?"

Morgan nodded. "Yes, he did."

We rode back in and called the sheriff. After old Tom was arrested, Mr. John went to the jail to see him and asked him why he took the colt.

He told Mr. John that after he'd been run off the farm, he was angry and wanted to get even. That Fourth of July, we'd been at the old diner. That's where Old Tom overheard us talking about how fast Little Brother was going to be. So, he thought he would take him and sell him for himself, get a wad of cash for him. But after he stole Little Brother, everyone around looked for a stolen colt. That's when he realized he couldn't sell him to anyone locally.

The few people from outside county lines that Tom convinced to come look at Little Brother only laughed, saying he was no racehorse prospect. He's was too small.

I asked Mr. John why Tom thought he could get away with such a thing.

"Stay away from alcohol, son," was all Mr. John told me. I was just flattered that he called me "son".

The night Little Brother escaped, Old Tom kept him in the shed after he attempted to dye him black. In another paranoid panic, Tom thought the colt was going to be discovered, so he decided that black was a good color to keep people from getting wise. But Little Brother kicked him hard on his shinbone and kept stepping on his sore foot, so

Tom decided to call it a night. He limped inside and drank himself into a stupor.

He didn't put any kind of reinforcement chain on the gate that night, so Little Brother, the escape artist, was able to break out. By the time drunk Old Tom woke up in the morning and went out to the shed, Little Brother was gone.

He was scared at first, but then said 'good riddance.' That's until the sheriff came knocking on his door. He said he was so sorry about taking the colt because he knew the colt was still nursing when he took him.

In the end, Little Brother sure got a lot of hugs and baths from Jane. And it wasn't long before all that dye was washed away.

Jimmy looked amazed.

"Little Brother was smart, wasn't he?"

"Yes, sir, I believe he was. Real smart, indeed."

Feb. 2nd

By this time, I had been at the farm going on two-and-a-half years, and I loved that place. I wished I could've bought it one day, especially the little house that Mr. John and Jane lived in. I considered Mr. John more than my boss; he was my first true friend. And I thought the world of Jane, and how she could ride. She scared me at times, just watching her ride. My goodness, that girl liked to go fast. She was a good friend of mine, too. My dad had told me if I had five people I could call friends before I died, I'd die a rich man. Now, I only needed three more.

Before long it was time to break the colts to ride. The year before, I was too green to help with the breaking part. I did all the saddling of the horses for the riders, and Mr. John said maybe the next year I could ride some of the easy ones.

Watching Mr. John and Jane work with those babies was like watching someone work magic. They took their time with them, but some of the two-year-olds were tough to break. And even if you did get them going you had to keep your eye on them. Those rascals can be unpredictable.

When it came time for Little Brother to get broke to ride, he acted like he'd been ridden all his life. I helped Jane ease up on his back, and he just stood there, waiting for her to give him a command. He was quite the gentleman, that little guy.

Within three or four days he was doing better than the other colts that had been in training for three or four weeks. It was like he naturally took to it.

His Big Brother, on the other hand, took more than five weeks to get going because he was so hardheaded. As soon as he was broke, though, he was shipped off to the racetrack. After he was in training for three months, he won his first race, equaling the track record.

Big Brother was on the trail to the Derby. The day it happened, that Craig fellow lost all his partners. They wanted to know how anyone could sell a colt like that for as cheap as he did and so early? Apparently, he was called lots of colorful names, most of it equating to how dumb he was. A short time later, I heard Rainbow Farms was up for sale.

At supper, Mr. John told Jane and me that he had asked some trainers about taking Little Brother to the racetrack. When they saw him, though, they all said he was too small and pigeon-toed. I asked Mr. John if he told them about the two brothers going head-to-head in the field.

"That was when they were babies," Mr. John said, "That doesn't mean anything for now. He'll have to prove himself again."

He went on to say, he had called an old friend in Prescott, Arizona, named Kent Roberts. Kent said he'd be glad to train him. Jane and I both spoke up at the same time, "Can't you find someone closer?"

John shook his head.

"Next week most of the two-year-olds will be gone from this farm," he explained, "and you two will take him there. I would like you both to stay and help Kent for the summer. After that, we'll run Little Brother over there and have us some fun."

Steve was looking at a win picture he'd pulled out of the box.

"Grandpa?" he asked, "Why doesn't this say Little Brother? This picture says Gallant Bill."

"Oh, yes," Morgan said, "Horses sometimes have lots of names, just like people. I have always called him Little Brother, but Jane called him 'Me, Too'.

That's because he always followed people around, wanting to get involved, being a pest. I'll give you an example."

One day, I was out in the field, trying to fix the fence. Little Brother followed Buddy and me out there. When I put my toolbox down, I looked back around and there he was. That little devil had scattered my nails and was holding my hammer in his mouth, waving it up and down. When I got my hammer back and before I could hammer a single nail, he had hung his head over my shoulder and was watching me. It always took me twice as long to fix things with him around.

I got smart later by putting carrots in my back pocket, and he would stay behind me, snacking. One day, though, the carrot got short and he ripped my back pocket right off. I had to chase him to get my pocket back before he swallowed it.

And he loved to stick out his tongue, have you grab the end of it, and play a sort of tug-of-war with it. But I already told you that part, didn't I?

Mr. John and Jane finally came up with a running name - Gallant Bill. Mr. John wanted to call him Bill after his dad and the Gallant part was because he had handled life gallantly, so far. Yes Sir, Little Brother was now Gallant Bill.

June 3rd

We loaded up Little Brother, I mean Gallant Bill. He just walked into Mr. John's old, two-horse trailer like he'd done it every day of his life. He even stuck his head out the side window, watching us as we loaded our gear into the truck, lazily munching on the hay from his hay net.

We said goodbye to Mr. John, and he promised he would see us in three weeks.

> Morgan leaned back in his chair and shook his head. "Oh my... I forgot all about this."

June 7th

We crossed into Arizona in the morning and Gallant Bill passed us on the highway.

Steve looked around like he didn't hear right. "What do you mean? He passed you? Was he running beside the truck? I thought he was in the trailer!"

"Okay... slow down... so, I can tell you."

We drove Mr. John's old truck and pulled that two-horse trailer, which we used around the farm.

Jane was sleeping with her head halfway out the window, her hair blowing everywhere. Buddy lay stretched out in the seat. I was half asleep, bored to death, plus it was hot.

At home, it was all green, but driving into Arizona, it was all sand and sagebrush with cactus. I began to think I was headed back to Texas.

Somehow, the latch that holds the trailer to the hitch came loose. Now, everyday everyone passed us on that trip. So, when I thought someone was going to pass me again, I slowed down a little and pulled a bit off to the side. But this time, Buddy barked his head off, scaring me half to death. I looked to my left and was looking Gallant Bill right in the eye.

His head stuck out the side window of the horse trailer, about a foot away from me. I could have reached over and touched him. He even had his tongue out.

The road was long and flat, but there was a slight bend, which let the trailer come beside the truck.

I yelled at Jane to wake up and that the horse trailer had come loose and was next to the truck. I immediately sped up and pulled in front of the trailer. I hoped I could slow it down before it crashed into someone or went off the road and rolled over.

Once in front of the trailer, I slowed it down a little by tapping the brakes. But, before I could stop it, we came to another bend in the road. This time it curved to the left, fast!

I didn't want to wreck us, but before I could make up my mind what to do, the dang trailer went off the highway.

It crashed through a barbwire fence, ran

through lots of sagebrush, and came to a crashing stop up against a big saguaro cactus. A few feet further, it would've gone down a 20-foot gully.

I slammed on the brakes, backed up, and drove through the hole in the fence. Before I could stop the truck, Jane flew out the door to check on Bill.

As I ran up, I saw Jane was grinning.

Jane stepped back to let me look for myself. Through the side door, I not only saw that he was okay, but he was playing with the hay net to let us know it was empty.

We didn't speak much as we were driving back through the hole in the fence and onto the highway. A few minutes later, we looked at each other. We shook our heads, started to grin and broke out in laughter, getting louder and louder.

"Wait till I tell Dad," Jane said. "He won't believe this."

"Do we have to tell him?" I asked.

June 11th

We finally arrived in Prescott.

Kent could now see that Gallant Bill was small, pigeon-toed, and car sick. It took Gallant Bill about a couple of days before he was well enough to go to the track and start training.

Kent eased his exercise rider up on Gallant Bill's back. When the rider started jerking Gallant Bill around and hitting on him with his crop, Jane yelled for him to stop that. The exercise rider jumped off and told her that he would like to see her do a better job. So, Kent told Jane to grab her helmet and show him, which she did. Gallant Bill walked onto the track and galloped around it like he was born there.

When Jane came back from the track, Kent told her that she had been taught well and gave her some more horses to ride. She also did great with them.

That evening, Kent pulled her off to the side. He told her that she was in a great place to learn to be a jockey, and that she should talk it over with her dad.

Jane told me later that her dad gave her a big speech about riding in races, his worries about her getting hurt, and her being his only baby. But she remained firm until he finally said that it would be ok.

Jane was raised around horses her whole life. She told me how her grandfather taught her to ride from the time she was just a little girl. She started with the easy ones first, till she could ride the tougher ones. With time she got better and became fitter until nobody had better balance on a horse. Jane was always the fastest out of the starting gate and could out-finish the other riders time and time again. When she also beat the ex-jockeys riding on the farm, people encouraged her to become one herself.

It was a good move for Jane to be in Prescott because she could ride a lot of races and learn faster there than in Kentucky. Being a girl in Kentucky was a disadvantage that gave her little chance of picking up a big barn to ride for. While the competitive spirit is a must, a jock getting started needs a lot of help and encouragement.

It was hard for women in those days to be jockeys. It was supposed to be a man's world. But, Jane would soon change that. She picked up race-riding quickly because she prepared herself well. Back in Kentucky, she watched every race film she could and studied the various race-riding styles of other jockeys.

She made some mistakes, too, but in Arizona people were more forgiving. It was a good place to learn, especially from Kent. He was a great teacher, even though he never got to ride in any of the big races. Still, he had ridden over 10,000 races with jockeys that would do anything to win. So, he knew all the tricks riders could use, like leg-locking, herding, or trapping a rider behind other horses, plus many, many more.

I once asked Kent if he had always wanted to be a jockey. He told me since he could ride when he was three years old, his dream was to be in rodeos. All he wanted was to be the world's best all-around cowboy.

His dad was a roper in the rodeos. At practice time, he would put little Kent on 300lbs calves he had just roped. Then, he'd turn them loose and let Kent ride them all the way down the roping pen. Kent was only 6 years then.

Those calves bucked, ducked, and dived all the way down there. At first, he was bucked off quickly, but as he got better, he rode tougher cows till at last, he could ride about anything. The hardest thing he said was to learn how to get off the cow at the end of the ride.

There is no easy way to get off a cow that wants you off. So, his dad taught him to roll into a ball and to never stop his fall by sticking out his arms, for that was the best way to break them.

When Kent was a kid, people thought he was a crazy guy who would try to ride anything. At ten, his family moved to Albuquerque, New Mexico. There, his uncle took him to see a man who was training racehorses.

Until then, Kent had never seen a racehorse. At first, he thought they were just unbroken horses, unlike his dad's roping horses that were taught to ground tie.

So, the trainer started him out by just walking them, and the horses would step all over his toes. Then, he had to ride bales of straw to get the feel of a different saddle and short stirrups.

Not long after that, Kent finally started riding racehorses. When he felt the power and speed in them, all he wanted was to be was the world's best jockey.

Kent said he would gallop any horse they'd let him on, and that they paid him 50 cents a head for it. He had a lot of spills from horses. But, riding those cows and remembering how to fall had helped him on many hard landings.

By the time he was 11, he was riding match races

on Indian reservations against squaws. The purse was sometimes around $50 and a couple sacks of grain. He told me that his dad had to lock him in the cab of their truck so the squaws wouldn't get to him and beat him up.

Later on, Kent told us he always dreamed of riding races with his dad. And years later, he did get to do that.

One day, he and his dad were riding races at Prescott Downs when in an earlier race someone had gotten slammed up against the inside fence. That rider knocked off the top board, and a repairman had just done a quick fix by laying it back in place. Five races later, it was time for Kent and his dad to ride. That's when a rider hit the fence in the exact spot as before. The board came loose and came flying towards Kent's dad at full speed. It hit him in the jaw and killed him instantly. This happened right in front of Kent. Kent said he could never get over that day, and it wasn't long before he quit race-riding and became a trainer.

Steve put his hand on Morgan's leg. "Grandpa was it boring being at the barns all day? What did you do at night?"

"Well, I met some interesting people.

One man I met was a crazy little guy called Art Blaze, the walking dead."

Both grandsons looked at each other and said at the same time, "The walking dead?"

Morgan got up from his chair. He put his arms out in front and walked around in circles, eyes half-closed, head tilted, and his tongue sticking out the side of his mouth.

Everyone was laughing, trying to figure out what he's doing. Even Buddy barked and wagged his tail.

Yes, Art, the walking dead... At night, we didn't have a lot to do. So, after eating supper, I went for a walk. When I saw a group of people, I sat down and started listening to their stories. Someone said to this guy named Art, "Why don't you tell Morgan about the day you got killed?" I looked around, and everyone was grinning.

Art told about his early days of riding. Back then, in California, they didn't have year-round racing. That's why a lot of trainers and jockeys went to race down in Mexico. The Mexican jockeys didn't like the American riders coming over and taking their money, though.

At the time, Art was one of the hottest jockeys

and winning lots of races. So, the Mexican jockeys got together and came up with a plan.

It seemed every time the riders would look over their right shoulder, Art was passing them. So, they planned to wait until Art made his move again. Then, just before he turned for home, one rider would hit Art's horse on its left shoulder. This would make the horse change leads and send Art to the outside fence.

It's called 'sending someone to the hotdog stand.' In Mexico, I guess, they'd call it a 'taco stand'.

Art's horse was at full speed when he hit the fence, sending Art flying through the air. He flew like that guy at the circus who comes out of that big cannon, shoots across the arena, and lands in the net. Except poor Art didn't have a net.

He went soaring through the judges' stand window, skimmed across the desk, and crashed into the wall. He almost put his head right through it.

Everyone thought he was dead.

One fellow came running into what was left of the judges' stand. He grabbed Art by his ankles and dragged him out from behind the desk.

Another concerned person grabbed Art by his wrist. Then both carried him out like a deer that had been hit by a car. Outside, they swung him onto the bed of a pickup and took off for the hospital like crazies.

Art was sliding all over the pick-up bed, bouncing up and down. He almost bounced out a couple of times, till a man put his foot on Art's chest to hold him down.

When they got to the hospital, they carried him again like roadkill and threw him on a stretcher. They told the doctor that Art was dead.

In those days, jockeys had a helmet that was made of tar paper. The doctor pulled off Art's helmet, which was pushed down around his ears, and took off his riding silks. They looked as if Art had walked too close by a hungry lion's cage.

The doctor also thought he was dead, so they put him in the morgue.

Minutes later, Art's girlfriend and other friends came running in, asking how he was. The doctors shook their heads and said they were sorry, but he didn't make it. They all left crying, and word spread fast through the grapevine that Art was dead.

While word was still spreading, Art, in the morgue, came to.

At first, he didn't know where he was or how he got there. There was a sheet over his head, and he slowly pulled it off. He looked around and saw other people covered in sheets with white tags on their toes. He slowly got up and walked out the morgue door, stiff like a zombie and still bleeding.

The door was difficult to open, so Art pushed real hard, making a lot of noise. The Mexican doctors and nurses, once they saw him, ran like heck out of there, thinking he had come back from the dead like a ghost.

Art walked out of the hospital and hailed a cab. The first cabbie that saw him drove off in horror, but Art caught another cab and told the driver to take him back to the racetrack.

The cab driver, seeing Art's blood, asked him to please quit bleeding on the seats.

Art got out of the cab once at the track and headed for the jocks' room behind the grandstands.

Just then, the announcement was made that word had come in that Art... was dead. There was a moment of prayer for him, and everyone stood with their heads bowed.

When Art walked by, looking like a bleeding zombie, more and more people saw him. The crowd began to gasp and point.

Finally, Art walked into the jocks' room. The jocks were still standing with their heads bowed, crossing themselves. Then, several jocks saw him. Their eyes popped wide open and their jaws dropped. Soon, everyone stared at him. That's when Art asked, all innocent: "Who died?"

>*Steve laughed. "Naw, did that really happen?"*
>
>*"Yep," Morgan laughed, " and that's exactly what I said to him. But, the others were nodding their heads. What can I say? Art later told me to come back the next night, because he had a thousand more tales."*
>
>*Morgan looked at the speechless boys. "OK, let's get back to the story."*

July 4th

It was the day of Jane and Gallant Bill's race. We'd been waiting a long time for this. I knew Jane was nervous, but I knew Gallant Bill would take care and watch over her.

July 5th

We finished in 2nd place. Jane rode a good race, and Gallant Bill got a little tired. But, he was okay. There was always a next time!

> *"Grandpa, tell us about that race! Was this your first time at the races?"*
>
> *"How close was the race?"*
>
> *"Yes, it was my first time at the races and there were about 100 or more people around the paddock."*

That day, Mr. John brought Jane her first new pair of jock boots, and Kent gave her his father's favorite race saddle.

Jane and I were both nervous in the paddock, but not Gallant Bill. He walked around like he owned the place.

The other two-year-olds were jumping around and were hard to saddle. I remember Kent telling Jane to relax and her horse will also relax.

"Just go out there and act like this is a morning workout," he said, "Instead of three or four horses with you, now you have ten."

In the race, Bill broke slow, and they got banged around a little leaving the starting gate, but Jane saw a hole along the rail and slid through to almost win. If it had been a longer race, we would've won it.

Still, it seemed that we had won that day with all the noise we made. Jane was so tired that we had to help her off Gallant Bill's back.

Kent was so impressed with her riding that it wasn't long before she was riding everything for him. Even other trainers started using her.

It took a while for the other jockeys to accept Jane. But day-by-day, she won them over because she hung in there and didn't act like a little girl. She rode as good as a man.

Oh, before I forget, a lot of cowboys were around that day in the paddock, but one man stood out. He was dressed in a suit, and his name was Sam.

He kept staring at Gallant Bill as if he knew him. He asked me out loud when I came to his side of the paddock from where in Kentucky Gallant Bill was from. Because in the racing form it said where a horse was bred, that Sam asked at what farm Bill was born. I told him. He claimed to recognize him because of the white marking on

Gallant Bill's forehead. It was in the shape of Texas.

That night after the race, Mr. John told us he had an offer to sell Gallant Bill, and we all held our breath.

That Sam fellow remembered because he came to buy foals at the same sale Gallant Bill's big brother went into.

He talked about watching the foals run and play when Gallant Bill tried to run with the others. He knew that Bill nearly crashed into the fence, before falling and sliding under it. And after Gallant Bill got up, how he was chased by the other colts. At some point, the two brothers had gone right past Sam and all the way around the field, head-to-head. He had also watched Mr. John and me scoop Bill up right before Craig came driving by to pick up Big Brother. Sam even asked that Craig why Gallant Bill wasn't turned out with the other colts and whether he was in the sale. But, that Craig told him Gallant Bill wasn't for sale and he was only a runt.

Finally, Jane asked her dad if he sold Bill. Mr. John shook his head. Sam offered him $10,000 cash, but there was no way Mr. John would sell him now. We were just starting to have fun, and besides, we were on the long road to the Derby. Wasn't that right?

Both Jane and I were able to breathe again.

July 15th

Jane and Gallant Bill raced again. I was going to put $100 on his nose to win. I'd been saving it for that day and sure hoped he liked mud because it was raining cats and dogs.

Steve looked through all of Bill's win pictures, trying to find his first. "Did he win? How much did you make?"

"Yes, we won. Gallant Bill broke slow again. The track was a sloppy mess, but he ran around the whole field to win. He went like a pig through slop going for his supper. After the race, Mr. John said Gallant Bill was a true mudder."

The boys cheered.

"We celebrated that night, and I told everyone that I made $500, which I sent to my girlfriend. Remember her?"

The boys shook their heads.

"She's the girl I tried to tell you two knot-heads about a few minutes ago. I

know your dad still wants to hear about her."

"Can't you go on with the story, grandpa? Please!"

"Oh, well then…"

That summer was great for me. Gallant Bill won his next four in a row and I loved that place. But Mr. John soon sent me back to the farm in Kentucky while they moved out to California. From there, Jane sent me the win pictures and newspaper clippings that are in that box right there.

I didn't see them again till after Mr. John told me they were going to run in the Kentucky Derby. I nearly fell over. I never realized until then that Gallant Bill was this good.

Even though Mr. John said they were going to be 99-1 odds, I didn't care if Gallant Bill came in last. I just wanted to see them all again.

I also read about Handsome Profit, Gallant Bill's big brother, winning five races in a row. In his last race, he even equaled the track record again. He was written up in all the media as the horse to beat in the derby.

"Grandpa, were you sad that you didn't get to go with them?"

"A little, but I had things that needed to get done at the farm."

But before I left for Kentucky, I met a boy named Joey. Joey was a want-to-be jockey who Jane met there. He was a really sad case. Mr. John and Jane left us going to California, and Joey stayed with me for a couple of days. After that, he was heading home to Boston to get some things. Most of all, he wanted to tell his mother that he was in love with Jane and about his dream to make it as a jock.

He told me how difficult it had been to grow up with his parents. His dad was a doctor, who everyone loved, but his mother was a pain. She always criticized his dad in front of anyone who would listen, and when she started drinking everyone just ran.

September 7th

Another letter from Jane arrived. The Sam fellow flew out to California to watch Gallant Bill run and win his fifth straight race. Now the Sam fellow offered her dad $50,000.

Mr. John still didn't want to sell and set him straight. Sam was wrong to think we were too much in love with Gallant Bill, or that we didn't know what kind of horse we had. All Sam tried to do was to buy Gallant Bill for bottom dollar after he proved he could run and was on the road to the Derby.

Jane also found that the newspapers and racing forms were now kind to her. They were all saying what a good job she did, riding with the best jockeys in the country. She also met some famous people, including some movie stars.

Morgan turned a page, and an old letter fell out.

"What's that, Grandpa?"

Morgan picked it up and stared at it

for a long time.

"*Is it from Jane?" Jimmy wanted to know.*

Morgan nodded. "Jane wrote lots of letters when she went out to California. She told me how things were going and what new things she saw. There were famous jockeys she met, and that she was finally at the real races. I kept her letters for a while, but eventually threw them away, except this one."

"Why'd you keep this one, grandpa?"

"I should've thrown it away a long time ago, too."

Now Jimmy was curious. "Grandpa, what did Jane say?"

Morgan moved around in his chair. "Well, before we get into that, let me first give you a little background on her."

Jane grew up fast as a little girl. The moment she got off the school bus, she took care of her mother and then the horses. She was always cleaning stalls or helping with the mares and babies. Hard work was part of her life. She didn't get much of a chance to date in school.

One time, she did have a date for the prom. She was so excited when this boy, who she liked quite a bit, asked her. She went to town and bought a pretty prom dress that she worked so hard to buy. Then, just before her date arrived, one of the mares went into hard labor. Jane cried and told him how sorry she was, but she had to stay home and help her dad. That boy got mad and never called her again.

During the summer in Arizona, she had a lot of free time on her hands, a first in her life. Other men were paying attention to her, but she met that young man called Joey, who also wanted to be a jockey. He was the one who came from a wealthy family that lived in Boston. His father had died when he was a very young boy, and his mother was too busy to raise him. So, he spent a lot of time with the gardener.

The gardener would take him to town, and, on the way home, they would often stop at the racetrack. That's where Joey learned to love horseracing and jockeys.

He went so often that the jockeys came to know him on a first-name basis. On his 16th birthday, the jockeys threw him a party, and he told them how he wanted to become a jockey, just like them.

They told him he needed to go to the smallest racetrack to learn how to ride races. There, he could make mistakes and it wouldn't be held against him. Then, after getting some experience, he could come back to ride with them.

One jock even had a friend in Arizona that would help him get started. Joey thought it over, went home, and tried to find a way to tell his mother about his dream. She always wanted him to be a lawyer like her father. When he told her his dream, she got angry. She told him he would never amount to much. He'd be a bum and an embarrassment to the family.

Joey always thought his mom was the reason his dad died in that car wreck. After his parents had their typical evening fight, his dad crashed against the very tree he told his close friends about that night. After that, Joey's mother ran the family with an iron fist. She thought Joey should be held back like a baby. He always had a nanny to do just that.

When Joey and Jane met on the backside of the track, Jane liked him right off the bat. Joey was funny and made Jane laugh. She was finally in a situation in her life when she could loosen up a little. She wasn't a stable-hand anymore, but a jock, and that required a lot of getting your head into the game. Jane was also turning into a woman. She felt good about herself as she had suddenly more time to enjoy life.

Every day, Joey would come by the barn to see if Kent would let him work a horse, galloping or letting a horse run a little, at times with another horse beside it. He hoped it would lead to a horse he could ride in a race. Kent didn't think he was good enough to ride his best horses. Still, he let him ride his cheaper horses because Joey was a good kid who tried hard. Plus, Jane liked him and that's who Joey really wanted to see and talk to.

    The two would work the horses together. Sometimes they'd go very fast to teach the horses to run next to another horse. A couple of times I saw her let Joey win the morning workout. Kent also saw it and told her that it wasn't good for the horses or Joey. They started hanging out more every day, and then one day, I saw that look that people have when they are in love.

    Joey never got the chance to ride the races Jane did. Still, he'd come along and watch her fight the jocks that squeezed or pushed her around in a race. A couple of times Jane had to tell him that she had to handle the other jocks herself, or the other jocks would become worse. It made sense, though - Joey just didn't want anyone to mess with his girl.

    He was very protective of her, and Jane tried to make him feel important. I once overheard her ask Joey if she had made the right move in a race, and

I thought she might as well ask me, for all the riding Joey did.

Then, Jane came to me and wanted someone who she could talk to about love, but, heck, all I could do was listen. What did I know about it?

She told me they used to go for hikes in the hills, holding hands, hunting snakes, or climbing rocks. One time they got caught in the rain and took cover in a small cave. There, he put his arms around her to keep her warm. She could feel his breath on her neck, and she felt a feeling she had never experienced in her life. She turned to talk to him, and they kissed for the first time.

He was proud of her riding abilities and wished he'd had her upbringing around horses. It's was sad, but very few trainers would ride him because he was over 5' 8" and he had a weight problem. I don't mean the kid was fat. He was just too heavy to be an effective jockey.

In those days, a lot of jockeys took reducing pills, and so did he. Even in 112 degree heat, he would put on a rubber suit and ride around in a car with the heater on to sweat off extra water weight.

He told me one day that the pills made him act a little goofy sometimes, but he thought it made him fit right in with the other jocks.

Morgan held the letter "Now, we'll have to talk more about this letter later, okay? But here it is."

Dear Morgan,

Today is the worst day of my life. I got three letters this morning.

Before Joey would follow us to California, his mother wanted him to come home for her birthday. She wasn't happy about Joey wanting to become a jockey, and she was especially unhappy that he wanted to leave to be with me.

The first letter I opened was from his mother. She told me Joey was dead. She wrote that when he came home, he looked so awful and thin that he almost looked like a different person. But he didn't just look different, he was acting awfully strange, too; he was nervous and couldn't settle. She said it was all my fault since I was all he talked about besides some silly races he rode in. Because he was so nervous, she called her doctor to look Joey over. The doctor put him in the mental hospital for a checkup. That's where he died.

She blames his death on me. Do you think it's true, Morgan?

The next letter was from Joey, but it was within another letter from the gardener named Juan Garcia.

In Joey's letter, he told me he wished he hadn't gone home for his mother's birthday but come to California with me. His mother insisted he must see her, and he wanted to pick up some of his stuff anyway. She had made a big fuss over how thin he was and wanted her doctor to look at him.

She, of course, also wanted him to give up the idea of becoming a jockey and us being together. She found the entire thing absurd. He was supposed to go back to school and become a lawyer for the family.

When the doctor looked at him, he wanted to know how he had lost so much weight, and why he was so nervous. Joey told him he was taking reducing pills, and their side effect was making him a little jumpy. Because the doctor wanted to know the reason for taking these pills, Joey began going on about his dream to become a Jockey. The doctor had no interest or concern for his aspirations and, very coldly, the doctor said he would never be a jockey, solely because of his size. It meant absolutely nothing to him that Joey had already ridden some races.

Anyway, Joey told me how much he loved me, and that being with me was the best summer of his life. All he wanted was to be with me as soon as he possibly could.

The last letter I got was from Mr. Garcia. He

told me he saw Joey every day, and that he was the only one who ever came to visit him.

Joey told him all about me and that he would marry me one day. His true dream was for the two of us to ride races together.

Joey tried to talk to the doctor and explain that he was okay, and all he wanted to be was a jockey. The pills were only to help him stay light, and that he would quit them as soon as he would start riding more races.

According to Mr. Garcia, Joey had been tricked by his mother. She spoke with her doctor and insisted that her son was very ill. She said I had been manipulating him to try and become a jockey with me even though he wasn't the size he needed to be in order to achieve such a goal. Because of this, she told him that Joey had become very depressed, and that she was scared he was losing weight to die.

He was only supposed to be in the mental hospital for a few days of observation, but his mother convinced the doctor that he needed to be signed in for an another 14. Joey was livid. He tried to fight and escape, but they put him in a cell and strapped him to his bed. The last time Mr. Garcia saw him, he was in that cell, and he felt unfathomably betrayed by his own mother. Nobody would listen to him, and he was so ashamed to be told that he belonged there.

Joey gave him his letter to mail to me, but Mr. Garcia also wanted me to know how Joey died. He said that Joey was certainly jumpier than usual, but he had still seemed happy, but after he was admitted into the mental hospital he changed. His smile had gone extinct, and all he saw was gray. He insisted that I not know where he was; he was ashamed to be declared fit for such a place. Joey wasn't allowed to call anyone and nobody there would truly talk to him; they smiled and responded, but they didn't truly listen. His mother, despite sending him there, never visited. On the evening of the day Joey was to be put on suicide watch, a nurse found him hanging.

Mr. Garcia talked to the nurse. The cell had a low ceiling so that people couldn't hang themselves, but Joey was able to pull himself up just enough so that when he tucked up his legs and let go, his neck broke.

Mr. Garcia was sorry to tell me all this, but he wanted me to know the truth.

Morgan, what am I supposed to do? I can't believe Joey is really gone. I thought we would be together somehow. We were a team; we supported each other through everything. Joey was always so happy to see me win, even though he never won a race in his life. He was just happy to be doing what he loved, with someone he loved.

The only other time I felt this kind of pain was when my mother passed away. I ride Gallant Bill tomorrow in the Santa Anita Derby, and, for the first time in my life, I would like to go and hide away from everyone. But I can't let my dad down by running away. Dad has been so good to me, and has supported anything that made me happy. He even said he hoped Joey and I would marry one day.

I can't wait to see you and hear your voice again, Morgan. I need a good friend now more than ever.

Love,

Jane

April 15th

Another letter from Jane arrived.

Dear Morgan,

We finished 3rd in the Santa Anita Derby, and it was a great race. Gallant Bill ran his heart out and got a little tired. I also met more famous people, and that Sam offered dad $100,000 after the race. Again, dad said 'no.' But, Morgan, that's a lot of money! He could even put a bid on the farm. If something happens, God forbid, dad could lose everything. I feel so much pressure on me.

I miss you and can't wait to see you.

Love,

Jane

April 20th

It was so good to see everyone at home. We were moving to Churchill Downs in a couple days, to get ready for the big race. I couldn't believe that we were actually going to be in the Kentucky Derby!

May 1st

Churchill Downs was crazy. There were people everywhere. When they say Derby Week is wild, they weren't kidding. I was so glad to see everyone, and they all looked great. I didn't recognize Gallant Bill. He'd filled out like a real racehorse. He was still small, but watching him and Jane gallop around the track gave me hope.

May 2nd

The pressmen kept asking me a lot of questions about Gallant Bill. One even asked me what horse I was leading around. I wanted to tell him off.

Jane tried to look more confident, but I could see the pressure on her. She still wanted her dad to replace her with a better jockey. After all, she was only 17-years-old and hadn't been riding races for very long. But her dad reminded her that no one knew Gallant Bill like she did. And besides, we were all in this together. I thought he was right.

May 3rd

We were in the middle of the barn, and every day the pressmen walked past us to look at Gallant Bill's big brother. I had forgotten all about him until Mr. John told me that Big Brother was so far undefeated. He had nine wins and was the favorite. He still liked to run head to head with any horse, and then run them down. Mr. John said his new name was "Handsome Profit."

May 4th

I got a good look at Big Brother, now called Handsome Profit, and he was grand to look at. He stood about 17`3 hands tall. It was hard to believe he and Gallant Bill were twins.

That Sam fellow came by the barn that day and pulled Mr. John off to the side. They talked for about ten minutes. I saw Mr. John take a few steps back, walk around in a circle, then walk up to him. They talked some more before that Sam fellow stormed off.

Kent, Jane, and I waited to hear what Mr. John told Sam. The day before, Kent and I talked about what would happen someday. We both believed someone would end up offering Mr. John too much money, and Mr. John would have to take it. And, as it turned out, Sam offered Mr. John $500,000 for Gallant Bill.

Now, that's not a lot of money for a real Derby contender nowadays, but in those days, it was an unbelievable amount of money.

Kent told Mr. John he should take the offer. Gallant Bill was going to be a long shot to win the Derby, anyway. Plus, Mr. John could use that money to buy back his old farm, which was up for sale.

But what we thought didn't matter.

The three of us wanted to hear the details of what Mr. John actually told that Sam fellow.

Well, at first, he told him that he would talk to us about having a new owner. But then the Sam fellow said he wanted his own trainer and jockey for the Derby.

Mr. John had to think about that for a moment and weigh it against all he could've done with that money. But then, he remembered his dream he's explained to us that one night at dinner after we'd seen how fast Gallant Bill really was. He had almost forgotten about.

But it took this Sam fellow to offer all that money to make Mr. John realize his dream was happening. It was coming true.

So, Mr. John told that Sam 'thanks, but no thanks.' Everyone had come too far to sell out now.

It cost Mr. John $100 to nominate Gallant Bill for the Derby when he was a weanling. Now, it was starting to look like he was going to get his money's worth.

Jane came up to me and told me she'd been asking her dad to replace her with a more experienced jock. Some jock agents had actually been telling her dad that he needed to do just that.

Even the newspapers did their best to criticize her at every chance they could. One jock, who didn't have a mount for the derby, even paid a newspaperman $2,000 to write how Mr. John should use that jockey instead of Jane.

She just didn't want to be blamed if things didn't work out right. Let's not forget, boys, Jane was still only a teenager. However, Mr. John told her that we were all in this together. We started out this way, and we would finish it this way.

"I have all the confidence in the world in you," Mr. John told her, "I always have."

Jane hugged her dad then, tight, and I couldn't help but shed a couple of tears myself.

"Besides," Mr. John said, "who knows that little ol' runt better than you do?"

Later that day, a couple of men came by the barn. They had been watching and keeping up with Jane and Gallant Bill out in California. They loved her riding, and, if they had a good horse, they would want her to ride for them. That sure made Jane feel better.

May 5th

Only one day to go! Mr. John walked up to me this morning, giving me $1,000. He said it was money he bet for me on Gallant Bill while they were in California. It was crazy, but it made me think about betting it all on Jane and Gallant Bill's nose.

May 6th

On this night, I thought we lost everything. A fire broke out in our barn. Luckily, I was sleeping on a cot in front of Gallant Bill's stall. At first, Buddy started howling, which woke me up. I put a lead rope on Bill, and we were the first ones out. But it was 1:00 in the morning and nobody else was up yet. Seeing that it would take too long for everyone to get up to get their horses out, I did something, which I didn't want to do. Mr. John later said that I did the right thing, but it could have been bad, really bad.

"What was bad? What did Mr. John mean?" Steve demanded.

"Okay, I told you we were the first ones out and that fire was catching on fast. I immediately knew that all the other horses weren't going to get out if more people didn't help. So, I turned Gallant Bill loose."

Jimmy stood up. "What do you mean you turned him loose? You mean you let him go?"

"Yes, that's exactly what I did. Now, let me explain."

Jimmy sat back down, seemingly angry at his grandfather.

I was sound asleep when Buddy woke me up with the loudest bark that turned into a howl. I sat up, wanting to get after him for scaring the jeepers out of me. That's when I saw the flames.

I immediately threw my cot to the side, put a lead rope on Bill, and took him out of the burning barn. That didn't take any time. We were out in a flash. But, I had no place to put Bill and nothing to tie him to. I also couldn't wait for the other people to get up and going while the fire was spreading. But, there was no one around to hold Gallant Bill. So, I called Buddy over and told him to sit. Then, I handed him the lead rope. And so he sat there, lead rope in his mouth, holding Gallant Bill. I turned around and ran back to help in the barn.

If I hadn't done that, Buddy would've followed me back into the barn. That's for sure.

Inside the barn, I opened all the stall doors so the other horses could run out. One horse just stood there, so I put a lead on him. And as I was running out, I saw Big Brother in his stall, fighting with his groom. The groom was doing his best to put a lead rope on him to get him outside. But, Big Brother cow-kicked the groom, breaking the man's leg. By then, other people were up and helping. Lots of people were yelling and screaming.

After they dragged the groom out of the way, I lead the horse I was holding into Big Brother's stall. I ran around a couple times. Then, as I came out, Big Brother followed us.

I got three more horses out before the fire became too hot and I couldn't go back inside. Then, I looked for Gallant Bill and Buddy. They were gone and my heart sank. But eventually, I found them.

Our pony girl, Eva, carried Buddy and lead Gallant Bill up to me. She was awakened by all the noise and alarms. Then, she saw me put the lead rope into Buddy's mouth and run into the barn.

She had to look twice to believe what she saw was happening. She immediately rushed outside only to see Bill running through people and cars. Buddy hung on for dear life as he was slung side to side and flipped over in cartwheels.

When Bill ran around the corner of the barn, he was so fast that he came head-on with the fire truck. As he tried to dodge it, he fell and slid up to the truck while still slinging Buddy everywhere.

Eva said she could see the sparks from Bill's

horseshoes on the pavement. That's when she ran over and grabbed Bill, held on to him, and led him back to me. She had Buddy in her left arm because his hind leg was broken. When he saw me, Buddy slowly wagged his skinned-up tail.

"Was Bill hurt? Did he get burned? And what about the other horses? Were you scared?"

"Slow down, Stevie. No, Bill only got a few scrapes, but he was okay. Yes, I was scared. But there's more…"

Just before the fire got too hot, I went back into the barn for one last time. I wanted to get out as many horses as I could. It was dark because the fire killed the lights. The smoke was terrible.

Sparks were flying from the electric wires. The only light was from the glow of the fire. It was red, yellow, and a terrifying orange. And then the panic noises of the horses, which I'd never heard before, the cracking of the fire, and all that yelling. That gloomy mix of light and sound was just awful.

Some horses wouldn't leave their stalls. Others even ran back inside the barn, into their own stall, and died there.

The last horse I got out actually ran over me. It was getting too dangerous in the middle of the barn, so I had to leave the rest of them in their stalls.

"Grandpa, how did that fire start?" Jimmy asked.

"Remember that Craig fellow?"

"Oh, that guy." Jimmy and Stevie nodded.

Well, I saw that Craig fellow in the barn that night. It was very late, and he was poking around, looking at Handsome Profit. He was probably thinking about all he lost. A security guard chased him down, telling him not to have a lit cigar in the barn.

I heard him say to the security guard that his cigar was worth more than the guard made in a week. Pointing at me and Buddy, he asked why the guard didn't watch out for that black boy sleeping in the middle of the barn?

"I don't trust him," he said, "and why don't you get his mutt out of the barn, too?"

Then, that Craig rubbed out his lit cigar on the side of the stall and the ashes fell between bales of straw. That's what started all that destruction. Later, they charged that Craig fellow with arson and he went to prison. He even tried to blame me. I like to think he might have met a few brothers in the big house.

"Grandpa, you saved Gallant Bill's big bother? You were a hero!"

Morgan smiled. "Yes, I did. I saved Gallant Bill and his brother and seven others."

Jimmy looked up. "You were really afraid, huh?"

"Very much so," Morgan admitted, "I've always been afraid of fires. When I was a kid, my best friend Danny died in a fire because of me."

The boys were flabbergasted. "What?"

"Well, let me tell you."

One night, Danny's little sister ran up to my bedroom window, yelling for me to get up and come to help. As I rushed out, I saw the sky was all lit up by their house being on fire. I ran up to my friend's window and looked in. I saw him lying on his bed with his baby brother beside him.

I yelled as loud as I could for him to get up, but he didn't move. I wanted to dive through the window and grab them both, but I for some reason I couldn't. So, I ran around to his father's bedroom window to see if he could help. But I saw that his father's bed was surrounded by fire and he was lying on it.

I ran back around to my friend's bedroom window, but by that time the smoke and flames were already entering the room. That's when I knew I'd waited too long. I could no longer climb through the window and grab him and his brother.

I hated myself for being a coward. Later in the morning, the sheriff and the fire chief came. They said it looked like the father had gotten drunk again and gone to bed with a lit cigarette. I told the fire chief what I saw when I first got there. Then, I asked him if I could've pulled my friend out the window when I first saw him? Did he think I could have saved his life?

I could tell the fire chief knew how I felt, and he told me that I did my best. But I kept on pressing him. If I would've gotten them out, could they have survived? Was it my fault? The fire chief never let himself admit it, but I thought I could see in his eyes, for a split-second, a look that told me, "Yes, it was your fault they all died."

My whole life I've had to live with knowing that I was a coward. I was going to do my best not to ever be a coward again.

Steve's jaw dropped.

"How many horses died, Grandpa?" Jimmy asked.

"I think about ten horses died in the fire that night," Morgan said. There were three horses we were going to race with at the Derby, and one of them was a co-favorite. He was a speed horse like Handsome Profit. He was the only one that had enough speed to go head-to-head with Handsome Profit. He was the one that we counted on to kill Handsome Profit's speed. Now Handsome Profit had no one to go with and push him. Everything was going to go his way, again.

"But I'm getting ahead of myself. Let's get back to Gallant Bill just after the fire."

I put Gallant Bill in our pony girl's stall and went looking for Mr. John and Kent.

When they first heard about the fire, they got there as fast as they could. They thought we didn't get Gallant Bill out of the barn. That's because no one remembered seeing us get out, and they knew we were in the middle of the barn, which was the worst place to be. And I hate to tell you how sickening it was to see the horses that didn't get out.

I took Mr. John and Kent back to the pony barn where we checked on Gallant Bill and let him rest for what was left of the night. Later in the morning, Mr. John and Kent had a talk. They couldn't decide if they should run him. As I was walking him around before feeding time, some birds flew by, and he tried to kick at them. We all knew then, that he was okay.

Stevie tapped on Morgan's knee. "Grandpa, did you hear those horses cry out in pain? I mean, the ones that didn't get out?"

Morgan shook his head. "Stevie, horses don't cry out in pain like people and other animals do. They are the only animals that do not cry out."

When I was a kid, I heard about a famous horse, an old one, that pulled a fire wagon. This was the way before fire trucks. Back then, firemen would have four horses pull a water wagon and go as fast as they could.

The story goes that the horse stepped into a hole on the way to a fire. He broke his hoof clear off but kept on running. Only later did they discover that he bled to death while they were putting out the fire. He never made a sound. It's the same with horses in a race. That's why jockeys have to pull them up as soon as they feel that something isn't right.

I only saw a couple of horses get hurt bad, and not one of them ever cried out in pain. Now I know why they call them the noblest of animals. Whenever I hurt myself, it makes me think twice before I yell out.

"Grandpa, go back to the horse that broke his foot, I mean hoof. Did he really break it clear off?"

"Yes, he did," Morgan explained, "In those days, horses pulled everything from buggies to fire wagons and trolleys. They had to backtrack to find his hoof. He had stepped between the trolley tracks and wedged it. They took that hoof, and, out of honor to that horse, had it bronzed. Then they put in a glass case with a plaque that

talked about the courage and dedication to duty this horse had."

Morgan looked at the two boys. They were overwhelmed.

"Maybe we should stop for today," Morgan said, "This all seems like too much for you."

"No, Grandpa," Steve protested, "we're ok."

"Yeah, we're ok," Jimmy agreed, "Tell us some more."

"You're sure, now?" Morgan asked.

The boys nodded.

"Okay, let's move on."

May 7th

Oh, what a night it was. I still couldn't believe we had made it this far. At 1:30 that afternoon, we were still waiting on our race. There were only three hours to go. I was going to bet $1,000 on Bill's nose. My hope was that the next day I could write in this journal: 'We have won!'

"Grandpa, did you win? How much money did you make? No, how much would you have made if you would've won?"

"You boys are so impatient. Let's see..."

I led Gallant Bill over to the grandstands. The last time I did that was in Prescott, Arizona. Back then, there were only three or four hundred people at the races. But on this Derby Day, boys, over one hundred thousand people were there!

It was a madhouse. I saw all kinds of fancy hats and pretty ladies. People were pushing and yelling. I tried to keep clean, but it rained that morning and leading Bill to the track left me as muddy as pig.

I led Gallant Bill into the paddock, and a valet brought out Jane's saddle. After he was saddled, I walked him around the paddock some more.

I think Gallant Bill was as curious about the crowd as I was. He pricked his ears at the flashing cameras and snorted the air as he pranced next to me. Believe me, he was excited.

Jane came out with the other jockeys, and I could tell she was nervous. It didn't look like she was even breathing. Kent told her that this race was no different than any other race. There were only more horses around her.

"Go out there and have fun," he told her, "Remember that when you relax, he'll relax. He can feel your heart. Save him for that long stretch. Once he feels your courage he will give you his whole heart."

Mr. John gave her a leg up onto Gallant Bill.

"And one more thing," Kent added, "Keep an eye on Handsome Profit. Don't let him get too far in front."

I led Jane and Gallant Bill around the paddock. The ocean waves of people yelled to Jane, "Good luck! Go, get 'em! Show 'em what a girl can do!"

Finally, I led them both out onto the track.

"Hey, Morgan," Jane said as we were leaving the paddock. I looked up at her.

"Have fun." And do you know what she did then? That silly girl, she winked at me.

And boy, if you thought the crowd was loud before, it was nothing compared to what it became when I walked them onto the track. It was roaring when I handed Gallant Bill off to Eva, the pony girl.

I had a friend who worked as a janitor in the Turf Club who let me come up the back stairs and onto the roof. And that was where I watched the race with a pair of ship binoculars I'd won in a card game a couple of nights before.

"Grandpa, what could you see up there? Was it scary?"

"Well, I could see everything," Morgan explained, "The horses seemed small because we were so high up. The people looked like a mass of ants on a drop of honey. The infield was packed and the band was playing. It was a one-hundred-thousand-person party.

"I watched Bill and Jane warm up.

Then, the horses start to load into the starting gates. They had to use two gates because twenty-two horses were running."

"Twenty-two horses? Where was Gallant Bill?"

"He was in post position twenty, the worst part of the track because of the rain."

Jimmy stood up. "What about Big Brother? Handsome Profit? Where was he starting?"

"That lucky dog had post position four. He had the best part of the muddy track."

Stevie also got on his feet. "Grandpa, where was Gallant Bill at the start? Was he in front with Big Brother? How far was the race?"

"Well then, let me tell you about the race." Morgan waited until the two boys sat down again.

As you know, I stood up there watching everything. I was on pins and needles. There was Jane, walking into the starting gate, Gallant Bill being the gentleman that he always was. Some of the other horses were giving some trouble to the pony girls and boys, especially Handsome Profit.

That big dummy treated that starting gate like it was the first one he'd seen in his life. Once all the horses were finally settled in the starting gate, it felt like forever before the starter pushed the button and the gates flew open with a bang.

Bill stumbled right away, and Jane nearly went over his head, but they quickly recovered. I thought Bill was almost last, but it was almost impossible to tell with so many horses running. His big brother was easy to see - he was in leading the field. Then, I saw Gallant Bill further back. He had only four horses to beat as he went into the first turn.

When Jane came by the wire for the first time, her blue and white racing silks were already brown with mud.

"Oh, you wanted to know how far the race was. It was a mile and a quarter."

"Yes, grandpa, but keep on going, please"

Morgan smiled at the two boys. "You really want to know?"

Jimmy and Stevie shouted together, "Yes, Grandpa!"

"Okay, okay!" Morgan laughed, "I'll tell

you what I remember."

After the race, Jane told us that when she went into the first turn, a wall of mud came back at them. She could barely see. She only had four pairs of goggles on, but before she got to the backside of the track, she had already pulled down two. Big Brother was way in front when they passed the half-mile pole. At that point, it seemed like Jane was hopelessly beat. I even quit looking through my binoculars. My heart sank and I honestly thought I was going to cry.

Well, going down the backside, Jane knew that she had to make a move soon or she would never catch up. But, how could she do that and still hope that Bill had enough strength left for the run down the stretch? After all, that was where it counted.

One-by-one, she started to inch by those horses. When she reached the three-eighths pole, she had to pull down another pair of goggles. That's when she saw that there were six horses still in front of her, not four. But Gallant Bill was hanging in there, and she felt like she might be able to catch a few more.

Seeing them at the three-eighths pole, I had a glimmer of hope and started praying. But, when Big Brother turned for home, he was still in front with only two horses close behind him and Little Brother wasn't one of them.

An old jock who stood beside me told me Big Brother's jock made a smart move. Even though he was in front of the field, he could still control the race. Any horse making a move on him would first have to get by those two riders behind him. The old jock grinned at me and said, "I hope your horse likes mud."

A grin spread across my face. I told him, "As a matter of fact, Gallant Bill loves mud!"

Meanwhile, Big Brother was saving a lot of ground compared to the other horses. Being on the inside, he was running a mile and a quarter. Everyone else, including his little brother, were running an extra fifty feet farther. That was like Big Brother getting a fifty-foot head start.

Jimmy stood up, protesting. "I don't want Big Brother to have a head start."

Morgan chuckled. "It can't be helped, that's racing, son. That old jock also told me that smart jockeys use the noise from the crowd to find out if someone is making a move on them. It's one of the best clues. If the crowd sees a horse make a move, they scream. If it looks like that other horse is going to run you down, the crowd goes crazy."

"Grandpa, did Gallant Bill make his move?"

Morgan smiled. "Sit down, and you'll find out."

The boys hit the floor.

At the quarter pole, Jane told us, she had only three horses in front of her. Two horses were real close, and Big Brother was far in front. She knew if she tried to go through on the rail, she'd be cut off. If she tried to go around, she'd be packed out wide. Those two riders knew they weren't going to catch the leader. They wanted to keep their places and would never share any ground. After all, second and third places were better than forth. The jocks took a quick glance at Jane. They must have known she couldn't see well because her last pair of goggles was packed with mud.

That's when Jane pulled down that last pair. Mud now peppered her eyes. When those two riders saw her without goggles and trapped behind, I'm sure they thought she was done for.

But you know what she did? That brave girl did something a rider normally doesn't want to do. She took a big chance. She slid Gallant Bill's head and then his shoulders between the two horses and split those riders. This was the first time being small paid off. I tell you, it was like a watermelon seed being pinched between your fingers and Gallant Bill shot between those two and was in front of them in a split second.

That move let Jane make up three lengths. I thought the crowd was loud before, but now, I could feel the grandstands shake under me. It was now going to be a two-horse race all the way to the wire. The whole place was going wild, and I was the loudest. I was jumping up and down, screaming my head off.

Oh, let me not forget what Jane also told us. Before that moment, she had been too busy riding to even think of Big Brother. But as she was drawing up beside him, she remembered when she was with him as he was born. How she loved him also, even stayed with him, while his Little Brother was put in that outside pen. She marveled that the two brothers had never been allowed to play together. They were separated and sent different ways, only to end up there together again.

Jimmy was almost in tears now.
"Please, Grandpa... Did he win?"

Passing the sixteenth pole, they were now head-to-head, stride-for-stride, and eye-to-eye. This was exactly what Big Brother liked. The crowd was now so loud that all I could hear at that moment was the hum of the tractor. It was pulling the feed cart in which I was riding two-and-a-half years before. It was that duel when I first saw the two brothers going head-to-head all the way around that field.

Up till that time, I'd worried about Mr. John. What was he going to do with that little guy? We just didn't know that it was going to take time for his small body to catch up with his big heart.

Suddenly, the old jockey next to me yelled, "Look how fast they're running!" He pointed at the timer on the odds board. He screamed that they were going to set a new track record.

That's when he said, "Boy, look at 'em! They're running a hole through the wind!"

Jimmy ran around like he was a racehorse. Steve, grabbed and pulled his grandpa's sleeve. He yelled at the top of his lungs, "Did he win?!"

Bill smiled and whispered into Margie's ear, "That's my Dad. He was always good at keeping me impatient."

Morgan saw that he had the two boys

at the point where they were ready to jump out of their skin. Taking extra-long, he turned to Margie. "I think, I could use a little more tea, please." He smiled at the boys.

"Well, there were 30 yards to go," he continued, "and Jane did something she was not comfortable doing. She switched sticks."

"Switched sticks? What's that?"

"Well, that's what they call changing your whip from one hand to the other, and it's hard to do. It takes years to master doing it smoothly and with confidence. At first, she didn't want to try it - take a chance and then drop it. It could have cost her the race. You know, people would've never let her forget it if she'd done that.

"But in a split-second decision, she switched her whip from her right hand to her left hand because she knew she needed one last surge of speed from that little runt. So, she popped Gallant Bill on his behind to keep him flying. That tiny love tap was enough to get Gallant Bill to give him the last of his heart. And do you know what that meant?"

Both boys, wide-eyed, shook their heads.

"That meant Little Brother burst forward and put his nose in front of Big Brother right at the wire."

Steve and Jimmy leapt up.

"He won?" Jimmy screamed, jumping up and down.

Laughing, Morgan nodded his head. "He won!"

"He won!" Steve repeated, leaping around like his brother. They both shouted it over and over again for what seemed like forever.

"Did you rush down there, Grandpa?" Steve finally asked.

"No! I couldn't move. That old jock had to help me up. Everyone around me was patting me on the back and hugging me. The crowd was like a raging ocean storm. It seemed like it took me an hour to get down to the track. The whole grandstand was crazy!

"I was so glad Jane took her time to come back to the winner's circle. I could barely walk. I met her and Bill at the finish

line and led them through the crowd to where Mr. John and Kent waited. When I led Gallant Bill and Jane into the winner's circle, Mr. John walked up and put his arm around me. He said, 'You know, this is only the beginning'.

Now Morgan's whole family wanted to know, "Is this the Kentucky Derby win picture? Did you feel like you were on cloud nine?"

Morgan stood up. The old feeling from the past made him teary-eyed.

"You know," he said, "I owe it to Little Brother and Jane that I was able to buy this farm. I bet my $1,000 on them that day. I was able to buy this place from Mr. John and marry my first girlfriend, then raise this crazy kid."

He pointed at his son.

"Didn't you know? She's the one I tried to tell you two knot-heads about. She's your grandmother, Edna."

"Grandpa?" Jimmy asked, holding up the jar with the rose inside. "What's with this?"

"Well," Morgan began, "Getting a horse like Gallant Bill is like catching

lightning in a jar. And I knew I would never actually catch lightning in a jar, not really. So, I took this from the blanket of roses that hung around Gallant Bill's neck in the winner's circle and I put it in my own jar. It will always remind me of what all of us truly had. But then, I did get my lightning in a jar when I married your grandmother. I only wish she was with us now."

Steve rubbed his head. "Grandpa, what did Mr. John mean when he said, 'This is only the beginning?'"

"Well," Morgan said, "the next time you two knot-heads come see me and bring me some more pecan pie, maybe I'll tell you the rest of the story."

A bolt of lightning flashed across the afternoon sky, followed by an immense roll of thunder. Two baby horses out in the field beyond leapt at the sound, bucked, and took off running. They bounded together, neck-in-neck, as quick as that lightning bolt.

"Look there, boys," Morgan said as he stood up to watch the two colts. His grandsons stepped to the edge of the porch to watch with him.

"What do you think?" he asked.

"They look like they could run a hole through the wind, Grandpa," Steve said, mesmerized by the speed of the two babies.

"That they do," Morgan said, "And what about you, Jimmy? Do you think there might be another Little Brother out there?"

"Yep. I think so, Grandpa."

Morgan put his arms around his two grandsons.

"Me, too," he said.

The End

About The Author

Raised around cotton, cows, and horses, Alan Patterson was in the saddle at the age of 3. By the time he turned 5, he wanted nothing more than to become a World Champion Cowboy. After his family moved to Albuquerque, New Mexico, Alan began to ride racehorses and, at the age of 10, started to compete in match races. At the age of 17, Alan became a professional jockey.

The Vietnam War interrupted Alan's horse racing career. He joined the Marines and saw combat in Vietnam. As his company's "tunnel rat," Alan distinguished himself and was quickly promoted to Sergeant.

Back home in the United States, Alan continued to ride professionally again. His highly successful career spanned 28 years, and he rode at 74 racetracks. Riding injuries finally forced Alan to retire.

In 2003, Alan made his motion picture debut when famous jockey Chris McCarron asked him to be the stunt rider and double on the Oscar-nominated film "Seabiscuit." On the set, the movie's stars, Jeff Bridges and Elizabeth Banks, urged Alan to turn his adventurous life on and off the racetrack into a book. Following their advice, Alan began to write what is now "A Hole Through the Wind."

Contact Alan Patterson:

AHoleThroughTheWind@yahoo.com

Made in the USA
Columbia, SC
07 November 2021